UNDER
THE
Mistletoe

Gay Romance Erotica

AMY REDEK

About the Publisher
4Fun Publishing, a member of **BLVNP Incorporated**, 340 S. Lemon #6200, Walnut CA 91789, info@blvnp.com / legal@blvnp.com
NOTE: Due to the highly emotional reaction of some people to works of erotic fiction, any email sent to the above address that contains foul language or religious references is automatically deleted by our anti-spam software and will not be seen. All other communications are welcome.

DISCLAIMER
Please don't be stupid and kill yourself. This book is a work of FICTION. Do not try any new sexual practice that you find in this book. It is fiction and not to be confused with reality. Neither the author nor the publisher or its associates assume any responsibility for any loss, injury, death or legal consequences resulting from acting on the contents in this book. Every character in this book is over 18 years of age. The author's opinions are not to be construed as the opinions of the publisher. The material in this book is for entertainment purposes ONLY. Enjoy.

Under the Mistletoe
Gay Romance Erotica

By: Amy Redek

© Amy Redek 2014
ISBN: 978-1-62761-8892

WOULD YOU believe that it was a sprig of mistletoe that changed my life? I was then eighteen years of age, but before we get to that, I'd better fill you in prior to this.

I was born and raised in Harrow, London and lived with my mother and father in a nice big house for we were quite well off. My father taught English at my local school while my mother, at the same school, taught French and Domestic Studies, i.e., cooking.

They had met at college with my mother being an exchange student from France. They fell in love and got married and managed to secure a place at my school as teachers. I came along two years after their marriage.

My grandmother on my mother's side, being alone in France, came over and lived with us and looked after me in my early years while my mother was at school. So I was brought up speaking both French and English.

It was also through my grandmother and mother that I spent a lot of those years, helping, if that's the right word, in the kitchen and so came to love cooking, especially the cuisine of France. Needless to say that when I did come to attend the same school that my parents taught in, I used to always come at the top of the class in the Domestic Studies and French, though not so good in all the other subjects.

I wasn't bright enough to be able to sit for a university place, much to my parents' dismay, but I had shown this remarkable talent for cooking. I professed that this was what I wanted to do and they agreed to fund my education in Derwent College, which was basically a school for aspiring chefs located in Stanmore.

So at the age of eighteen, I left home to attend this college for the next two years. It wasn't really a college per se, but an old hotel that had been adapted to take in twenty students a year, ten boys and ten girls. This was the limit because the old hotel only boasted thirty rooms on two floors so it was a matter of doubling up with the girls on the first floor and the boys on the top floor. The two male teachers had their own rooms on this top floor and the two female teachers had the same on the first floor along with the girls.

The top floor also housed the two porters, one on the day shift and one at night. They also acted as the security guards. On the first floor lived the two cleaners, the school secretary did not live in the school.

***

Upon entering the college through the main door, there was a lounge off to the left with a small bar that we found was tended by one of the teachers on a rota basis. Off at the end was the office. On the right from the hall was the dining room that had been shortened in length by having the kitchen moved up from the basement, which now served as a preparation room as well as having the freezers down there as well as a small bakery. This was also used as a classroom as was the actual kitchen.

***

At my initial interview, it was noted that I spoke fluent French as well as being brought up by a domestic's teacher which resulted in my acceptance into the college as well as being able to afford the fees which was quite high.

It was because of my French that I was paired off to share a room on the top floor with Georges Roznoir, an English born boy but of French parentage. He explained to me later that his family had traced their name as far back as Agincourt where one knight had on his shield a black rose. The latter being spelt as roz in French, whereas the noir was black when translated into English, hence the name, but that was as far as they could go for they couldn't find out his real name as he was always known by his shield.

We were introduced in the lounge on our arrival, telling us that we will be sharing a room. I was taken by him from the start as we were about the same height and quite good looking, though with tongue-in-cheek, not as good looking as me.

It was a mixed bunch as it goes in respect of nationalities, which was good as we would also be able to learn some of their own countries specialties while they learned ours. The pairings had been made and after we were given our room numbers, we all trooped up the stairs to find them and get settled in.

Georges and I, with our suitcases in hand, found our room number twelve and went in.

'Well, Rosie,' I said as I dumped my suitcase down on the floor. 'Our home for the next two years.'

Instead of using his Christian name of Georges, I'd used the play on the first part of his surname and since he wasn't objecting, it became the name he got known by among us. By the same token, I didn't mind him shortening my name of Nicholas to either Nick or Nicky.

It was nice to note that as the place had once been a hotel so it contained its own bathroom with the usual facilities, just inside the door on your right as you entered the room. Past this and off to the right were two single beds with a small table between them with a lamp on top. Hanging from the ceiling between the two beds was the main light with a horrible coloured shade. Opposite the beds was a small dressing table with mirror and a chair either side. The wardrobe was built into the wall up against that of the bathroom and opposite was the window that looked out over the street below.

'Which bed would you like?' I asked of him as we surveyed the room.

'It doesn't really matter, Nick,' he said. 'A bed's a bed,' as he sat down on the first one, giving a little bounce on it. 'This one will do.'

Which pleased me for I would then have the one closer to the window and would be able to catch the breeze first in the height of summer. So I put my suitcase on what would be my bed and opened it and began getting my things out. There were two drawers either side of the dressing table, which was as good a place as anywhere for my underpants, socks and handkerchiefs. I hung my trousers and jacket on the right hand side of the wardrobe and found that it also had drawers for shirts and T shirts. Footwear went onto the bottom while toiletries went into the bathroom.

As instructed, when we'd finished unpacking and our suitcases put under the beds, we went down to the lounge to be told the rules of the college. There were too many to list here and there were groans from some of the boys to learn that the bar was only open from eight till ten in the evening and that drunkenness would not be tolerated. If we did want to stroll round the town in the evening, we had to be back inside by eleven o'clock. Also the girls were forbidden at the top floor and the boys the first floor at all times. Any female caught in a male bedroom would be expelled immediately, the same for the boys if caught or seen coming from a room of a female.

'No fun to have here then,' said Rosie in a whisper to me.

'But they didn't say anything about when we're outside,' I whispered back to him with a grin. Though I didn't think the girls would go for having it somewhere outside when it was cold, which was a bit of downer for me seeing as I was still a virgin when it came to having sex with a girl.

***

We also learned that it was the second year students who prepared and cooked all the meals, taking it in shifts. This first year was about being able to know all kinds of fish and meats. How to pick the freshest and learn how to cut joints and gut fish and really start at the very beginning of the culinary art. This also included the art of baking and making pastries, etc. Though there were some like me, that had been brought up in this way, there still would be a lot to learn.

***

Our first dinner there was café style but at par with any good hotel in its presentation and taste and I enjoyed it. Rosie and I had two beers at the bar in the lounge afterwards before going up to our room and bed. We had to be up for breakfast at eight for our lessons would start at nine. When in the second year, our start in the morning would be six o'clock to prepare the breakfast if it was our turn.

This was to be my first night away from home and to share a bedroom with another person, though I wouldn't have minded it if it was a girl. Rosie, I learned later, had a brother and so wasn't as shy as I was in undressing in the presence of another male. With his clothes off and placed on the chair on the left of the dressing table, he went off into the bathroom to brush his teeth and have a pee before getting into bed. I saw, in his nakedness, that he had a prick and balls about the same size as mine and as he was prepared to walk about near like this, I soon lost any inhibitions about him seeing me fully naked.

I'm not ashamed to admit that I did shed a few tears into my pillow that first night, it was my first time away from home, but soon got over that as I had fun for the rest of the year.

***

I learned that Rosie's family owned a bakery in Barnet, just north of London and this was his speciality in the confectionery line whereas mine was in French cooking. It's all very well in the cooking and preparation of these meals but it was here that I really learned how to first cut the joints of meat for me to be able to do it right by the joint or chop.

During that first term, we were mixed on a frequent basis, each learning what we knew from the other and I got on quite well with both the girls and the boys, and before we knew it, Christmas was upon us and we all pitched in with our Christmas dinner that turned into a grand little party in the bar to round off the last night before the holiday.

The lounge had been gaily decorated with chains, balloons, streamers and mistletoe. With there being several sprigs of the latter, many couples kissed underneath it. I think I got to kiss most of the girls of both years during our drinking session over the two hours that the bar was open. I also surprised myself by how much I drank in those two hours too, for I was quite tipsy when the bar finally shut down.

Rosie enjoyed himself too for he was in much the same state as I was and he even stumbled as we went upstairs after finally saying goodnight to those still in the lounge. It was in this state that I pulled down one of the sprigs of mistletoe and took it up to our room. We bounced off several walls on our way before falling into our room.

We both sat on the ends of our beds as we took off our clothes, throwing them in the direction of the chair opposite until we were naked. I then stood up and with the sprig of mistletoe in my hand, got up onto my bed and straddled my legs to stand on and fixed it on the horrible lamp shade that hung from the ceiling.

I nearly fell over when I got down but was satisfied to see it hanging there and beckoned Rosie to come over to me as I now stood beneath it.

'I haven't wished you a Merry Christmas yet,' I slurred. 'Come and give me a kiss.' He stood up, nearly falling over and came round between the beds and into my arms. 'Merry Christmas,' I said and held him close to me and we kissed.

Boy! That was some kiss we gave each other, arms tight around the other, pressing not only our lips, but our bodies up close and we both got the same reaction. I could feel his cock rise up and hard, the same as mine between our tightly joined bodies. Both our lips seemed to part at the same time and our tongues met and began to move against the other as the kiss became prolonged. I think we were both conscious of how our cocks were throbbing being tightly squashed between us but neither of us seemed to want to break off the physical contact we were having. But we did.

'Christ!' we both said in unison as our bodies came apart, looking into each other's eyes, trying to see what this kiss had meant, but I couldn't see what he was thinking and I don't think he knew what I was either. Our outstanding cocks were still touching each other as our hands were still in contact with our upper bodies.

'I've got to get rid of this,' I gasped as I moved away and went past him and into the bathroom, my cock, up hard and throbbing, painfully I might add. I leaned my left hand up onto the tiled wall above the toilet and used my right hand to jerk myself off, which didn't take more than a few strokes for me to start shooting my sperm out and into the toilet bowl.

What a relief that was but it had also put my mind in a turmoil. I had kissed quite a few of the girls when down in the lounge but not one had the reaction that I'd just had in kissing of Rosie. The thought of any kind of homosexuality between us never entered my thoughts at this time and so I gave my now deflating cock a final shake before going back into the bedroom.

Rosie was now in bed and his face was screwed up, his eyes closed and I could see that his hand was under the covers by his stomach and knew that he had just finished in jerking himself off. His body had reacted the same as mine at the contact and I wondered just what were his thoughts were at this time.

I got into my own bed and turned off the lamp and settled down but not in my mind as I tried to get a grip with how my body reacted to that kiss. I fell asleep while still stroking my now flaccid penis. As I said at the beginning, it was that sprig of mistletoe that started things off.

***

Nothing was said between us in the morning when we got up and saw to our ablutions before getting dressed and packed before leaving to go to our respective homes for Christmas.

Goodbyes were said to all the others with the wishes for a merry time and also a happy New Year as we left the college to go off to the station for the train. That was the Bakerloo line though I had to change at Wembley Park onto the Met Line for Harrow. Rosie had got a taxi for this would be far quicker for him than trying to get to Barnet by underground.

***

It now seemed strange to get undressed on my own and not have Rosie there opposite me as I got into bed and turned the light off, not saying goodnight to him that evening. In the darkness there, I then thought of the kiss we had and how both our bodies reacted to this. It hadn't happened when I kissed the girls under the mistletoe but it had with him. Just this thought had brought my cock up to a full erection and I slowly rubbed it as I thought of that kiss again.

I pushed the covers back so that I had my cock upright in my hand as I moved the outer skin up and down the shaft, loving the feel and wondered if I would react the same way again if we kissed. The next minute I was rubbing myself hard and gave out a sigh as my cum shot up all over my stomach and lower chest, squeezing hard to get the last drops out before fumbling for a handkerchief to wipe myself clean. With another sigh, I pushed the handkerchief under my pillow and dropped off to sleep with the thought of kissing Rosie again when we returned to the college.

***

It was a lovely Christmas again, me helping mum do the main dinner and was not denied having some wine with them at the meal, well I was eighteen and allowed to have a drink now and then. Even though we had central heating in the house, we still had an open fireplace and we burnt the traditional Yule Log on Christmas Eve.

Logs were burnt on New Year's Eve too and a few days after this, mum and dad went back to work while I still had a few more days before it was my time to leave for the college. The parting wasn't so bad this time when I kissed mum goodbye and shook dad's hand and it wasn't long before I was back in my room at the college.

**

I was there before Rosie and saw that the mistletoe was still hanging from the lampshade before I unpacked my suitcase. It wasn't long before he turned up and we wished each other a Happy New Year before we went down for our dinner that had been cooked by the second year students that had to start on as soon as they had arrived.

We had a couple of beers in the lounge before we went up to our room, nearly everybody turned in early. We sat, as we usually did, at the bottom end of our beds to undress, throwing our clothes onto the chair opposite. I was naked first and sat down near the top of my bed until Rosie walked round where I then stood up and faced him, standing under the sprig of mistletoe.

'We had a Christmas kiss under this,' I said as I looked up at the sprig hanging there, making him glance up to it. 'Shall we wish each other a Happy New Year the same way?' I said somewhat shyly. We looked into each other's eyes, a small smile on his face as he nodded and moved into my arms and our lips met again in our second kiss.

Holding each other as we went into a clinch, the fronts of our bodies met as did our pricks and, as before, with this close contact as we kissed, our pricks became rampant cocks again, being squashed between us.

'Oh Christ!' I said as our lips parted but with us still pressing our bodies against each other. 'It's happened again,' I managed to say in a strangled voice.

'Mmmm,' he murmured as the tip of his tongue came out and moved across the lips I had just kissed. My cock throbbed even more as I saw this for it was so erotic in my mind then.

'I've got to get rid of this,' I stuttered as I pulled free from his arms and went off to the bathroom and jerked off into the toilet bowl. He did the same as last time, by laying in his bed and I saw that he had just done the same though it must have been into a handkerchief.

I quickly got into my own bed and turned off the lamp but I couldn't get off to sleep, thinking of that kiss again and it wasn't long before I was up hard again.

'Nick. Are you still awake?' I heard Rosie whisper.

'Yes,' I whispered back, still slowly rubbing my second erection.

'I...I've been thinking about the kiss we had,' he said.

'So have I,' I replied, feeling a tremor run through my body.

'Would...could we have another,' he stuttered, 'I liked it.'

'So did I,' I said with a tremble in my voice.

'Will you get into bed with me so that we could have another one?' His voice low as he asked this.

'Yes,' I said, my heart thumping as I pushed my covers back and got out from my bed and moved that short space across to his.

He'd pushed down the cover for me to get in alongside him, our bodies touching and I could feel the heat that his was giving off. He couldn't help but feel that I had an erection as I turned on my side towards him, it getting squashed up tight to his thigh.

My arm went across his chest as in the dim light coming in from the window, I could see that his eyes were shining and saw him give his lips a touch with his tongue.

'Oh Rosie,' I groaned as I then moved right over and on top of him, feeling that he was as hard as I was. His arms came round my back as I moved my head down and our lips met once again in a kiss.

There was passion from both of us as we kissed, mashing our lips against each other until they parted and our tongues gave both of us a kind of an electric shock. My cock was really hurting me now as our tongues played with each other and I began to move my body up on his, feeling our cocks rubbing together as I moved.

'This is lovely,' he murmured as I moved on top of him and I gave him another kiss before speaking.

'If I keep doing this, I'm going to come all over your stomach,' I said.

'Then let it go for I'm nearly there now,' he replied and raised his head to kiss me again. I leaned my head forward to push his down as I kissed him back and began to really move myself up on top of him. I could feel his hard cock rubbing against mine between our stomachs and loved the feel of where it was and kept moving, getting faster as I reached my peak and began to shudder as I came. I could feel it squishing out between us and knew from his movements under me that he too had come at the same time, smearing our joined sperm between us.

We both gave out a sigh as I slowed down and could feel the sticky mess making our stomachs slippery.

'That was great,' he said as his hands came up to the sides of my head and pulled it down for him to mash his lips tight up mine in yet another kiss.

'It was,' I said when he released me. 'But let me clean up the mess we're now in,' I said as I eased my body up off of his, hearing a squelching noise as we parted.

I got off the bed and went into the bathroom and wet a flannel and wiped the mess of our cum from my stomach and cock before rinsing it and taking it back into the bedroom. He was still on his back, his deflating cock still on his stomach as I wiped the mess from this and ran it over the head of his cock.

'Get back in,' he said hoarsely as I finished, so dropping the flannel on the floor, got back into bed with him. Here we both rolled onto our sides and kissed again and just kept stroking each other's body until we fell asleep.

***

It was strange to wake up feeling another body next to mine and my morning erection pressed up tight to his back. It didn't take long for it to sink in where I was and my hand moved over his thigh and felt that he too had an erection and gave out a small groan as I grasped it firmly and began moving my hand up and down on the hard shaft.

'That's nice,' he murmured. 'Don't stop. Just keep going.' I realised that he would come all over the sheet if I did so, so I quickly released him and rolled the other way to be able to reach down to the floor and pick up the flannel. He'd given out a groan when I had released him and had now rolled over onto his back so I had to shift my body so that I was almost hanging out over the side of the bed.

He was smiling up at me as I took hold of him again but now with the flannel over the head of his cock as I resumed jerking him off. It didn't take long before I felt his thighs tighten up as he began to spend himself into the flannel. His eyes were closed as he sighed and knew that he had finished.

'My turn to see to you now,' he said as he shifted his body for me to lie down on my back, my cock hard and throbbing now up and laying on my stomach.

How lovely it was to have a different hand from mine doing what I like being done to my morning erection. Having been really aroused at doing it to him, I was soon bucking my hips as I came in the flannel that he'd put over the head.

'Just lovely,' I said, breathing out at just having another wonderful experience of being seen to by someone else in this fashion. He leaned over and gave me another kiss before saying that it was time we got up for a shower.

***

It seemed a long day before we were back in the lounge to have our beer and getting a secret smile from Rosie as we sat together with the others, talking over the day and it wasn't long before we left the lounge and went up to our room.

It didn't take long for our clothes to be taken off and it was Rosie who went and stood under the mistletoe for a kiss before bed. Our bodies met at the same time as our lips and had our upright cocks again being squashed between us.

'Can we do the same in your bed tonight?' he breathed out as our kiss was broken off.

'I can't wait,' I smiled back at him as we came apart for me to turn and pull the covers down and get onto the bed. He smiled back at me as I opened my arms for him to get on and in between them, lying on top of me this time. It was nice to have his body on mine, feeling our cocks being pressed hard into my stomach. We kissed but much slower this time, still feeling the passion but without the mashing of our lips. These parted for our tongues to touch and tease as my arms held him tight round his back as he began to move on top of me.

It was wonderful having this experience of another person on top of me, feeling our cocks moving between us.

'I'm coming,' I managed to gasp out between our kisses.

'So am I,' he grunted and this time I was able to feel his seed start to coat my stomach along with mine as he still moved on top, pushing himself down hard on me as we released the pressure from our balls.

He moved his body sideways after we had finished, still kissing and feeling our sperm getting smeared all over my stomach.

'My turn to do the cleaning up,' he said, giving my nose a kiss before easing himself up to the noise of our bodies parting. His cock, still hard, swayed nicely as he moved to the bathroom to get the flannel.

I lay there looking down at the mess we'd made on my stomach and ran my fingers down into it and got quite a lot sticking to them. Now what made me do what I did next, amazed me, for I then stuck these sticky fingers into my mouth and sucked off the mixture of our two lots of semen.

There was a slight taste that I couldn't put a name to and even went and took some more from my fingers and sucked this off too. I was still sucking my fingers when Rosie came back into the room with a damp flannel to wipe me and I somehow felt somewhat pleased with myself for having done what I had and wondered what a mouthful would be like and if I could then identify what the taste was.

He wiped me down before putting the flannel on the side and got into bed with me, where we kissed and cuddled each other till we fell asleep. This then became the pattern for us every night, taking it in turns to be the one on top in our respective beds. I again, when I was underneath, would sample the product from our balls by taking scoops of it to try and work out what the taste was.

The pattern was changed about three weeks later.

***

Down in the lounge was a vending machine that sold a variety of things, and on this evening, Rosie bought a chocolate ice cream bar to take up to our room. He went and put this down on the dressing table before we took our turns in the bathroom, brushing our teeth, etc.

Our undressing routine was the same and when naked, we kissed under the mistletoe and it was several minutes before we broke this off.

'I forgot my ice cream,' he said, moving over to the dresser and peeling off the top half of the wrapper. 'Want a bite?' he asked as he sat down on his bed, breaking off the end.

'No thanks,' I said as I sat down opposite him as I watched some of the ice cream start to drop off the end.

'Bloody thing's melting already,' he said, catching a few drops and taking another mouthful. I watched this as suddenly, a small lump of this ice cream broke away from the bar and landed squarely on the top of his erect cock. 'Hell!' he mouthed as I watched that blob of cream start to slide off the head.

Now I don't know why I did what I did then, but I slipped off my bed onto my knees and went and caught that blob of ice cream with my mouth. Though it wasn't just the ice cream that I took in, but nearly the whole length of his cock.

I felt the blob slide down my throat but also felt the heat of his body that had melted it and with this loose cream moving about, sucked it off, using my tongue in the process.

Rosie had given out a gasp as the cold ice cream landed on the partly exposed flesh of his cock and then a second gasp as my mouth closed over it. Now he gave out a groan as I sucked on him, while I got a queer kind of feeling in the pit of my stomach at what I had suddenly found doing. I felt my face flush at what I was doing and lifted my head up to see what I had just sucked on as if it was the first time that I had looked at it.

I looked up at him and saw that his head was thrown back and his eyes were closed but what I noticed more was the fact that he had actually clenched his fist and now his ice cream was dripping all out from between his fingers. He must have grasped it hard when I had taken the head of his cock into my mouth and had squeezed it hard enough to half melt and now drip down to the floor.

'Wow!' he exclaimed, opening his eyes and looking down at me before noticing what had happened to his ice cream. 'Shit!' he now cried out as he stood up, his cock bouncing nicely before my eyes as he moved round the bottom of the bed and off to the bathroom. He must have thrown the rest into the toilet for I heard it flush and then the running of the basin tap.

'That was just great, Nick,' he said as he came back into the room. 'Will you do it again in bed?' he asked as he pulled me up and kissed me. It took a moment for me to break free and give out a shaky laugh.

'If you want,' I said, 'though I'll want you to do the same to me.'

'That I will as I liked it, so I think you'll like it too,' he said as he turned and got into his bed, holding the cover up for me to get in alongside him. This I did and went into his arms for our kisses and my mind was in a whirl that I was shortly about to move down the bed and take him into my mouth again.

After a few minutes, we broke off and looked into each other's eyes and smiled. I then gave him a quick peck on the lips and moved slightly and kissed his chin and began to move slowly, kissing my way down his body. Butterflies were flitting around in my stomach as my tongue rove down over his, feeling the head of his cock touch the side of my head.

I moved mine and looked at the fiery head of his cock, twitching away, it partly exposed by the forced back foreskin and I gave my lips an unconscious wipe with my tongue before opening my mouth and taking him back inside once again.

I heard the groan he gave out as I used my lips to push the foreskin right back so that I had the bare flesh under my tongue as I moved it round the head. I felt his stomach muscles tighten up when it stroked over the G-spot but couldn't suck on him properly until I had more saliva in my mouth. So for a minute or two, I let my tongue continue to stroke the flesh of his cock head while my hand just gently moved the skin up and down the hard shaft.

With enough saliva in my mouth, I moved up onto my left elbow to be able to hold his erection upright and was then able to bob my head up and down on the head of his cock as I rubbed the shaft harder. I felt his thigh start to go rigid as he gave out another groan.

'I'm coming, Nick, I'm coming,' he gasped and I held my lips tight round the base of the head as his hips started to jerk towards my bobbing head. His cock seemed to swell a little bit more as I felt the first of his coming come up his cock and have it erupt in my mouth. Not one load, but several, filling my mouth completely. It nearly made me gag as some started to slide down my throat but held most of it there till he stopped his bucking and only then could I swallow what was there.

It went down smoothly until I only had the residue there to find that the taste was slight but not unpleasant, and carried on licking all 'round the head, gently squeezing to get the last drops out before lifting my head up to see the big smile on Rosie's face.

'That was fantastic, Nick!' he exclaimed. 'Was it as good for you as it was for me?' he asked, his eyes really shining.

'You'll find out,' I said with a grin, feeling rather pleased with myself for what I had just done and now realised that my own erection was up hard and really starting to pain me. 'Now shift over so that you can see to me in the same way.'

He moved himself over onto his side so that I could lay down flat and when settled, he leaned over and kissed me the same as I had done to him and then began to kiss his way down. I couldn't help but give out a tremble as his hand took hold of my cock and hold it upright in his hand. He turned his head and gave me a smile before turning back to lower his head and take my throbbing cock head into his mouth.

I gave out a gasp as it was taken into the heat of his body and gurgled with delight when I felt his tongue move over the top and felt the foreskin being pushed back. It was glorious to feel the movement as it caressed the bare flesh and closed my eyes at the pleasure I was getting. I was loving the way his hand, the first one to ever handle my cock in this fashion, was holding it tight and rubbed the soft skin up and down on the hard muscle beneath.

It wasn't long with his hand movements and his sucking that I neared my peak, and like him, had gasped out that I was about to come.

'Mmmm,' was all I got in response except for him grasping me tighter and moving his hand a bit faster and I gave myself up to the pleasure as my hips began to move up to meet his bobbing down head and started to send my seed up into his mouth. It was lovely. Very lovely indeed. The bonus I got was the fact that he was fondling my balls at the same time. He must have swallowed my coming for he didn't let go of me for several minutes as he kept on sucking and squeezing. He finally lifted his head up and gave the top of my cock a kiss before moving up the bed and into my open arms for a kiss.

'That was just great,' he said, his eyes shining brightly after our kiss. 'We should have started doing this earlier.'

'What did you think of the taste?' I asked.

'Can't really say. It wasn't as unpleasant as I thought it might have been,' he replied.

'So you prefer us doing it this way instead of us rubbing our cocks up against each other's stomach then?' I asked.

'Oh yes! I enjoyed it. Didn't you?'

'Of course, my sweet,' I said, giving him another kiss as well as a strong hug, and it was with lying in each other's arms that we fell asleep.

***

We were now in the habit of sleeping together in alternate beds, which made the morning task of making it down to just the one bed being made up. This wasn't one of the cleaners job.

In our lessons, I noticed that we seemed to be handling more food in its raw state than we would be eating and learned the reason why. This surplus as it were, was made up into dinners that the college had a contract with an old people's home, and that the college prepared both lunches and dinner for the people residing there. This offset the cost of the food for us to learn on and not be wasted.

I also found that Rosie was simply a wizard at the art of baking, be it bread, rolls and pastries and other small delicacies that he'd learned from his parent's bakery. His vol-au-vents were first class. I didn't really have a specialty like this and that was why I was there at the college to learn.

We laboured away with things like a side of beef and have to cut out all the joints etc, until we only had the bare bones left which were used in some soups to get the marrow out. The only thing I didn't really like was the handling of a live eel and have to cut its head off before cutting it up into manageable pieces.

One of the main things I was not used to and that was how to prepare crab and lobster, which became one of my best dishes in the end. Crab sticks were a dirty word at the college.

So not only were we learning about food preparation and the serving up of such, Rosie and I were learning more about the erogenous zones of the male body at night. As I think I've already mentioned, we only slept in one of the beds at night, holding and kissing each other as we fondled the parts that we liked to use in our sexual couplings, though this was all oral at the time.

Taking it in turns to go down and take the throbbing erect penis of the other into our mouths to suck and gently chew on till we brought about the desired result. This eventually developed into where we would do it to each other at the same time. Top to tail, sucking and playing with the erection in front of our eyes and also found out that we could, later I might add, that some certain spices we could identify in the sperm as we rolled it round in our mouths before swallowing.

We would do this to each other at least three nights a week and we would also do it in the morning before getting up if we didn't oversleep, and before we knew it, it was half term.

As much as I missed my parents when I was at the college, this short ten day break meant not having Rosie sleeping with me and I found that I missed this more when in my bed at home at nights. Here I could only masturbate and think and imagine that it was Rosie doing it to me, but missing having him suck on the end of my pulsating piece of meat.

On returning to the college and going up to my room after this short break, I found that Rosie was there before me. As soon as I dropped my bag on the floor, he pulled me in between the beds and under the now very wilted piece of mistletoe where he hugged and kissed me. I think he missed me as much as I had missed him.

I think that this was the first time that we kissed under this while still wearing our clothes, which I might add, didn't stay on long before they were off and we both fell naked onto one of the beds and went down on each other.

It was just great to be lying on my side again and having his wonderful erect cock in my hand, pulling the foreskin down to reveal the flaming red head of his cock just waiting to be sucked and chewed. What a delight it was to take him back inside and suck and lick it all over, making him quiver as I touched the G-spot with my tongue and to also have the same being done to my throbbing erect cock. But now we also used our teeth to nibble our way up and down the solid shaft and sometimes take in the opposite pair of balls to roll around but without using the teeth on these soft plums inside their sac.

So we were into the last quarter of our first year there, knowing that in the coming year, we would actually be cooking the meals for the others, though on a rota system. Five groups of four will cook for the forty odd persons that lived in the college as well as the meals for the old people's home, for one week, and then assist for the other weeks. But I will come to the exams later as it applied to us.

This last part of our first year soon came to an end and Rosie and I made pigs of ourselves in trying to stuff our mouths as much as possible with each other's dick as we could manage, which should last us for the six weeks we would be away back in our respective homes. There actually were tears in the eyes of Rosie as we kissed one more time under the mistletoe as we said our goodbyes to each other, and seeing this, brought some to my eyes too.

***

Back home, mum and dad were delighted in the meals that I cooked for them, showing them what I had learned so far at the college and to justify what they had paid for me to do. This was my way of not paying for my lodging as it were, though they would never have asked me for any with me not really earning a wage.

The days I got through fine but it was when I would get into my bed of a night that I felt at my worse. I would nearly always have an erection and I would gently rub myself as I thought of Rosie. Rosie getting undressed and seeing his naked body before me, waiting for me to take him into my arms to kiss and press our naked bodies up tight against each other.

To feel his hard cock being squashed between us and then taking hold of it and taking it into my mouth to suck and chew on and get him to erupt and give me his semen to taste and savour before swallowing it.

I could also see in my mind's eye, his naked body as he went off to the bathroom, seeing the cheeks of his bum slowly move up and down in the motion of him walking. This brought on a craving that I would then like to be able to put my cock in between those ripe cheeks and fuck the arse off him. It was when I got to this point that I would then shoot my load all up and over my stomach and give out a groan that he wasn't there to suck on me.

As much as I liked being home, my heart was back in the college with Rosie. I thought so much about fucking him that I bought two dozen condoms and a pot of cream to take back with me when the time came. Mum thought it somewhat strange that I didn't go out some evenings to try and find a girlfriend, but was pleased that I threw myself wholeheartedly into giving them the best meals I could produce.

The first week of September came around and it was time for mum and dad to start back at their teaching posts in their school, leaving me at home alone for that one week before college started.

It was then that I realised that if it became possible for me to fuck Rosie, he would then want to fuck me in return. How would I react to be then playing the role of being the woman? This gave me food for thought, but not for long for as much as I liked having his erection in my mouth, I now wanted to know what it would be like in having it rammed up my backside.

Could I act the part of a woman for him to fuck? This chain of thought caused me to wander into my parents' bedroom and go through the drawer that held mum's lingerie. Just running my hands through what was there made me tremble and have the sudden desire to put some of it on. I carefully took note of how things were placed in the drawer before pulling out a brassiere and a pair of stockings as well as a suspender belt to hold them up.

I could hardly contain myself as I quickly stripped my clothes off and sat down on the bed and inexpertly rolled the nylon stockings up my legs. Boy, didn't I get a hard on in just doing this. It was sticking out in front and throbbing like mad, but refrained from touching it while in the process of putting on these female garments.

I had no chance of putting the clips of the belt into the hooks with it being behind me and so brought it round to the front and clipped it on this way before pulling it round my waist. I stood up and pulled up the tops of the stockings and put the studs into the clips. This took several goes, making the studs stay in place and hold the stockings up. My cock was bouncing about as I twisted my body around to be able to clip the side ones properly.

I decided to fix the bra in the same way by doing it from the front before twisting it around and then putting my arms through the shoulder straps before settling it down at the front. I used my socks to pad the cups out and when this was in place, I finally stood up and went and looked at myself in the wardrobe mirror.

It looked rather incongruous to see myself with these bits of female clothing on and have a massive erection sticking out in front of me that I almost laughed, but at the same time, got a vicarious thrill at seeing myself in this mode of attire. So much so that I actually began posing myself before this mirror, giving my mouth a pout to see just how I looked at different angles.

My hair was now quite long, not having had it cut for nearly a year, wearing it in a ponytail most of the time. But I now pulled it forward around my head to frame my face. This was really the first time that I had studied my looks and saw, not without some dismay, that if it wasn't for my cock jutting out like it was, I could actually be looking at a female posing in front of this mirror.

With this thought in mind, I went and sat down at the dressing table and used mum's brush on my hair, bringing more forward and around and saw that with a little make-up on, I would indeed look very much like a female and not a male at all.

With my erection really paining me now just looking at myself, I quickly got my handkerchief out of my trousers that were lying on the floor and posed myself before the full length mirror and jerked myself off.

Too many thoughts flashed through my mind in those few moments of jerking away at my cock. One being how Rosie would react to seeing me dressed like this. Would Rosie dress up like this so that I could think that it was a woman that I was fucking instead of a man? I had to overcome the first hurdle and that would be getting Rosie to bend over for me to fuck him.

Other thoughts ranged through my mind as I took off this clothing and carefully replaced it exactly the way that I had found it in the drawer. I mulled these over as I got dressed back into my own clothes and went downstairs and made myself some lunch.

I cooked dinner for my parents again that night and later, when I was in bed, I relived the thrill I had gotten in putting on that female underwear and jerked myself off again before falling asleep.

I dressed up every morning for the few remaining days of the holiday, loving the thrill and erotic stimulation I got from pulling up the nylon stockings and fixing them to the belt before parading myself in front of the mirror. With my hair brushed properly and wearing the bra, with my cock and balls pushed back between my legs, it looked as though I was actually seeing a woman reflected in that wardrobe mirror. I tried turning around to see what I looked like from the back, but couldn't do so without another mirror to look into, which we didn't have.

***

So it wasn't with any reluctance that, after saying goodbye to my parents, I went back to college. While sitting in the train, I gave thought to the condoms and cream that I had in my bag and the vision in my mind of the backside of Rosie. This gave me a massive hard on sitting there and had to really study the advertising panels opposite me to take my thoughts off of him and was fortunate enough to lose the tumescence before I had to get up to change trains.

It was only four stations on both lines and I was soon at Stanmore and out and making my way to the college. Here, I found that Rosie had gotten there before me again and it was a lovely welcome I got when I entered our room. His arms opened for me and went into his embrace as we kissed and welcomed each other back for our second year.

That was all we had time for as we were supposed to start right away into our new duties now being second year students. These rules or tasks, whichever way you looked at it, was that we were now responsible in the actual cooking of all meals for the students for this is our second year.

There was a rota system for only four at a time were in charge of the cooking of these meals with the rest of us assisting where and when needed. Rosie and I had been scheduled for the first night's dinner along with two of the others, both girls, for this was the kind of pairings that the teachers had insisted on. So we were on dinners for one week and then it would be breakfast and a week later, doing lunch. Then we would have two weeks as assistants before starting the cycle again.

So Rosie and I with the two girls did dinner that night. While the others dined, the four of us had our meal after the rest had eaten. By the time we had finished our meal, we only had time for one beer before the bar closed and two tired persons went up to their bedroom. But this didn't stop us from, when undressed and naked, having our ritual kiss under the now sad looking mistletoe before getting into one of the beds.

Here we went into a clinch and kissed each other, our hands caressing the other's body, not missing out on the erections that we caused to grow with our kisses and hand movements. It wasn't long before we were in the reverse position to be able to take the cock head of the other into our mouths to suck and gently nibble on.

How glorious it was to once again have his cock in my mouth to lick and suck as my tongue teased him till he erupted and filled my mouth with his cum. I had let go at the same time and we both could feel the semen being moved over the raw flesh of our cock heads before we swallowed the essence of each other.

Even while I was sucking on Rosie's cock, I had the thought running through my mind of how it would feel if it was up inside my backside. At this point, I was a bit on the shy side in bringing up the possibility of us both fucking each other and so carried on having the pleasure of his cock in my mouth while mine was in his without bringing the subject up. I did a week later when we changed over to the breakfast shift.

We had finished for the day and we only stopped in the bar for one beer and were soon up in our room where we got undressed. I think he looked forward to us being in bed together as much as I did, and found out a few minutes later that this was the case.

We had our ritual kiss under the mistletoe, pressing our bodies close up to each other, squashing our erect cocks up tight between our stomachs before we broke off and got onto one of the beds. Rosie's eyes were shining and he licked his lips before moving closer and kissing me as we nestled into each other's arms. Now was the time I thought.

'Rosie....Rosie,' I stuttered. 'I....I. Do you like what we do in bed here? Sucking on each other?'

'Oh Nick, yes. Of course I do. I couldn't wait to get back here to be in bed where we are now,' he said, kissing me again.

'Well, I wondered if you would like to take the loving we do with each other a, er, a little further?' I managed to get out.

'You mean the ultimate union between two lovers?' he smiled at me as he asked this.

'Yes. I've come to love you very much and I've found that just sucking on you is not enough. I want to fuck you and have you fuck me.'

There! I'd finally said it, and was a bit surprised when Rosie had a fit of giggles, squeezing me as he did so.

'I've come to love you too, Nick,' he said, 'And I think that our minds are in tune with each other, for I was having the same thoughts myself but didn't know how to say the right words.'

'You don't know the torments I went through the whole of the holiday, wanting you. Wanting your cock in my mouth, to suck and chew on and take your seed to taste and swallow.'

'Oh darling the answer is yes to both! I too want to make love to you in the only way that we can really show each other of the love I have for you, and that is to let you stick that lovely cock of yours up inside me. And if you love me as much as I have come to love you, you'll let me do the same to you.'

I think tears came to both our eyes at this double declaration of the feeling of love that we had for each other, and he surprised me again by adding some more.

'So much that I wanted us to get closer together, I even went out and bought some condoms for us to use, hoping against hope that we would be able to use them on each other.'

He really burst out in laughter when I told him that I too had bought a dozen of the rubbers with the same trepidations in mind as he had.

'Oh Nick, I'm so glad that you had the same thoughts as myself, for I didn't really know how to say what I wanted most in the world, and that was for you to fuck me. And,' he gave me a shy smile, 'That you would let me do the same to you.'

That was it that we both were of the same mind and thoughts and now we were about to bring ourselves that much closer in the only way that men could and that would be the joining of our two bodies into one as we made love.

Rosie pushed me back and rolled over to be on top of me, his eyes bright as he looked into mine.

'Will you fuck me first? I asked this for I'm frightened that I might back out at the last minute.' he asked this in a quiet voice and I pulled his head down and kissed him before speaking.

'Rosie. I've loved having your cock in my mouth, and all through the holiday I've had dreams of having the full length of you inside me. To give me the ultimate pleasure of us being together and that we are both of the same mind, I'll go first and then you can have me in the same way.'

We kissed again and I think that his erect cock was hurting him the same as mine was doing to me and he rolled off of me and reached out to the drawer of the bedside cabinet between the two beds.

'Oh shit!' He exclaimed. 'I've left mine in my suitcase.' I chuckled at this and had a job of speaking properly.

'Don't worry for I've already put mine in the drawer, as well as some cream,' I added.

So he pulled the drawer open and got out a condom and the small pot of cream and rolled back to me and lifted himself up to be on his knees to look down at my body.

'I've taken it into my mouth,' he said as he opened the wrapper and pulled out the condom, 'and just hope that it fits and that I will get the same pleasure that I had in sucking it.'

I smiled up at him before he lowered his head and took the head of my now really throbbing organ into his mouth for a quick suck. It was only a quick one to make it jump and twitch at his action before releasing me and then rolling the rubber down over the head and shaft till it was fully covered.

'You put the cream on,' he said as he moved over to let me rise up, well in the body sense I mean, for my cock was already up waiting to have this experience of fucking another male up the backside.

With me moving about, he was able to get into the middle of the bed and what a sight that was that came into view as I shuffled round and got in between his open legs. The cheeks of his bum there before me as I opened the cream pot and took out a blob, which I smeared over the head of the condom. I wiped my finger of the residue at the entrance to his backside highlighting the target which was now there on offer for me to realise what I had dreamed of during the holiday.

His bum was like a pale white peach, the cleft separating the two halves and the creamed orifice I was about to stuff my prick into. I shuffled closer till the head of my cock was an inch or two from the target before I paused and stroked both halves of this peach, the fruit of which I was just about to dip into. This stroking of his bum caused him to give out a shiver as he waited for this, the moment of truth that he was about to know what it meant to be the recipient of another man's love and need for him.

I put my left hand onto his hip as I held my cock straight with the other as I nuzzled the head to the entrance of his being and felt him give out a tremor as he felt the touch of my cock head to his rear end.

He muttered something which I didn't catch but when it came to my turn, it must have been something along the same lines of what he was about to receive, etc.

With the head of my cock firmly in place at his entrance, I let go with my right hand and held his other hip and pushed my body forward.

God it was tight! I could feel that he was using his sphincter muscle to try and stop the intrusion.

'Relax Rosie,' I said, still keeping up the pressure. 'Relax that bloody muscle.' He must have done so, for all of a sudden, I was sliding up into him.

What an incredible feeling that was to have the head of my cock suddenly be encased in his body heat, hotter than his mouth and then to get the same along the length of the shaft as that followed until my thighs were tight up against the cheeks of his bum.

Though my cock, measured from the base of my stomach to the tip was seven inches, I only got about six of them inside him for the cheeks of his bum prevented me from having the whole length of me up inside him, but six inches of a blood engorged cock was enough for him to what it was all about.

'Christ!' He gasped, the single word coming out in an explosion of breath that he'd been holding in as my thighs came up against his bum cheeks. 'That hurt.'

'Shall I pull out?' I asked, worried that I'd really hurt him.

'No!' He cried. 'It hurts at first, but now that you're there......Oh Christ! I can feel every throb of your heartbeat. It's incredible!'

But now that I was fully in, well as far as I was able to go inside him, I started to move myself backwards and forwards fucking him. He actually started to croon as I moved myself in and out of him, though out is the wrong word for it was more of a forward and backward movement, not the actual pulling out of him.

It was fucking great!

But the actual thrill of fucking him up the backside was short lived in this first time fucking anybody for I'd not yet had the pleasure of having a woman. Too soon, my mind was crying out as I quickly reached my peak as I moved my cock inside him in this mode of having sex. Too soon as I held him tight with my hands as I rammed myself hard up against his bum cheeks as I then gripped him tighter as I began to shudder, my sperm shooting out into the rubber as I came, in what felt like to me, the most I had ever expelled from my balls.

He knew I was coming, not only from my grunting but of the short sharp stabs of my cock as it was only my hips that were moving at this point as I came inside the man that I had now fallen in love with.

I had come and conquered as it were as I felt absolutely drained as I leaned over his rear end, panting heavily and saw, but had not felt, sweat dripping off my forehead onto his lower back. He was now gurgling beneath me, which quickly turned into a cry of alarm as I began to pull myself out of him. His sphincter muscle, instead of trying to stop my entry, was now gripping me, trying to prevent the removal of that piece of flesh that had invaded the very being of himself.

He gave out a cry as I finally left his body, he fell forward while I thought that I'd hurt him and quickly fell onto his back to try and soothe him. I was wrong for he was crying at the loss, he said, feeling the thing that had given him pleasure being withdrawn from his body and it wasn't until it was my turn did I realise exactly what he was saying.

But as I didn't get a coherent reply, I lifted myself up off of him and off the bed, on wobbly legs I might add. I went into the bathroom and used some toilet paper to pull off the condom and dropped the lot into the bowl and flushed it. I wet the flannel there and went back with it to wipe the residue of cream from his bum before getting back onto the bed to cuddle him.

He had rolled over onto his side for this and we were both almost incoherent in our speech as to how wonderful an experience it had been, he loved having me inside him and I said I loved him for letting me fuck him.

This lasted a few minutes before I moved up, knowing that now it was my turn to have the experience that Rosie had just had, of having a male organ pushed up inside of me. I had loved having it in my mouth but now was to be the test if I could take and love having it actually pushed up into my back passage.

I got another condom out of the drawer and as he rolled over onto his back, his face alight and his eyes, well, shining doesn't sound enough, for there was more meaning to the look that they conveyed and the one that seemed to be the most obvious was one of love.

Trying to hide the emotions that must have been showing in my eyes, I bent my head down and took the head of his cock into my mouth, that lovely cock, and gave it a few sucks before rolling the condom down until it was completely covered.

Words were not needed as I moved over to let him rise to his knees as I assumed the same position that he had been in, on my knees, bent forward, leaning on my forearms thus making my bum stick up. I flinched at the touch of the cold cream, much in the same way that he had done, and said a small prayer as I felt his hand come onto my hip and felt the head of his cock touch the cream at the entrance to my grotto.

My mind was telling my body to relax at the first pressure to my rear entrance, but the body was not reacting as the muscle there started to contract. This made the entry a bit painful as the head of his cock widened my back passage for the first time, but once the head slipped in, the rest of his shaft moved in smoothly.

Oh my God, it's incredible, my mind shouted out though it was a grunt that came out of my mouth. I'm sure that I could feel his heart-beat, throbbing away through his prick that was now fully up inside me.

'My God! It's lovely,' crooned Rosie, almost echoing my thoughts as he was motionless behind me which was somewhat aggravating by him not moving. All that moved were his fingers flexing themselves on my hips and his cock that was pulsating away but the bugger wasn't moving.

'Move Rosie, for Christ's sake!' I gasped. 'Let me feel it move.' This then triggered him off and he began to move his hips backwards and forwards, making his cock slide inside me.

It was incredible! Being able to not only feel the heat of his cock, but having it slide in my back passage, giving me a thrill as he did so. I found I was also drooling at the mouth at the wonderful sensations that rippled through my body by having him fuck me.

But like me, it wasn't long before his fingers tightened themselves on my hips and began to pull me back onto him as he began ramming himself tight up to my thighs, making a slapping noise as the naked flesh came together.

'Arggh,' he cried as he held me tight and stopped moving, just letting his cock throb and pulsate away as the sperm was ejected into the condom. I swear I felt his coming but that, I think, was just my imagination at the thrill I was getting of having him where he was now.

He too was sweating at the effort he'd put in fucking me, for I felt drops of it splash down onto my lower back as he leaned forward.

'Stay where you are, Rosie,' I grunted as I was now taking his full weight on my rear and lower back as I began to ease myself forward. His hands slid up my sweaty body until he grasped my shoulders as I became prone on the bed, lying on my front with him now fully on my back and still with his cock up my backside.

'Keep moving if you can,' I gasped out and his hands then slid under me to hold my shoulders from underneath and began rocking himself on top of me, his cock still up hard, moving at the same time. It was glorious!

But nature had its way and he was soon deflated enough for it to suddenly slip out to my cry at the loss of that wonderful throbbing organ that had just been giving me the greatest pleasure I had yet known. It was just as good having his cock there as it was in my mouth though I didn't get to taste his sperm this time. We sorted that out later for after we had fucked the other, the condom would be stripped off for the recipient to then suck out any residue of semen and finish off by licking the cock head clean.

But with this being our first time fucking each other, the condom was pulled off and dropped onto the floor as I rolled over onto my back and took him into my arms for us to kiss and tell each other at how wonderful it had been. We didn't do more than that on this night for with our shift at cooking had changed so that we had to be up and working at six in the morning to prepare breakfast.

***

Over the following weeks, we would either suck each other off or fuck one another nearly every night and before we knew it, Christmas was upon us again.

On reflection and looking back to that Christmas party we had, I kissed most of the girls under the mistletoe there but didn't get the slightest arousal from the kissing of a female and yet, just the touching of Rosie's lips would always bring me up to a massive erection.

Before we left the party, I acquired a fresh sprig of mistletoe to replace the sorry thing of last year that was still hanging down between our two beds and with this fresh sprig up, Rosie and I kissed each other and went and fucked as we gave each other our Christmas greetings and the present of having a cock once again shoved up our back passage. Not only that but a good slug of our sperm because for the first time, we had each other bare back. That means without using a condom and it was an even greater thrill to actually feel the semen hitting the inner passage when he came inside me. The drawback to doing it this way meant no sucking of the rampant cock until it had been properly washed, but by then, most times it had begun to deflate.

We both had tears in our eyes as we kissed our goodbyes in the bedroom before saying goodbye to the rest before we left to go to our respective homes for the Christmas break.

***

I won't say that Christmas was a bore this year, but it wasn't the same with not having Rosie there to see to my needs in the sexual content at night in bed. Also, there was only one day that I could raid my mother's lingerie drawer and dress up in this attire and masturbate while looking at my reflection in the mirror dressed in this fashion. I also tried for the first time to put on some of her make-up but didn't do a very good job of it and soon washed it off.

Christmas day passed and so did the New Year and it was time to return to the college for our final six months.

***

Christ! We'd only been in the room five minutes before we were both naked and I was on my knees having him stick his cock up my backside and take me to heaven in this glorious fashion. He loved it too when I got round to fucking him before we turned around and sucked each other's cock, not forgetting to pay homage to the balls that produced the sperm that we would taste and savour before swallowing. Girls? We didn't need them.

But now in this latter part of our course, we tried to put all we'd learned into producing mouthwatering meals for that would be part of our final examination. The first part was that each of the twenty students will be given a menu each, which was handed out at random. We couldn't see what the menu was as we picked them and found that half were for lunch and the other for dinner.

They were basically the same in the format i.e. soup, entree, main course and a dessert. These four dishes would be rated from one to five in points with an additional three that could be earned for the choice of soup and of the vegetables selected to go with the main course. So there would be a total of twenty-six points to be earned. Eighteen points or less would mean a failure. So with four teachers marking the meal that would be served to them meant that the topmost marks would be one hundred and four and if seventy two or less, you failed.

Now my menu for dinner showed the soup of my choice to be a compliment to the entree and main course. This also applied to the luncheon menus I found out, for Rosie had picked a lunch menu.

We got these a month before the end of the course, giving us one week to think on what and how we would prepare this meal and then take turns cooking and presenting this meal to the four teachers to evaluate, which started on the third to last week at the college starting on a Monday.

This would be done in alphabetical order and so I would do my dinner on the Tuesday of this first week, my surname being Craig, and Rosie would do his lunch on the Wednesday of the second week, his last name being Roznoir.

Rosie was in somewhat of a tizzy when he saw his and it wasn't till we were in bed that night that I could calm him down. For some reason, I don't know why, but when we were in bed together, we only spoke French. Well, I suppose it's the best language when making love to someone. It has a lovely purr when spoken softly into the ear that you are nibbling.

So with these whispered words, I kissed him, moving my body down until I found his erection and took the head of his cock into my mouth to suck and tease him. I then couldn't say these words for it's rude to speak with your mouth full. I loved to feel his legs tremble when I lay half across them as he neared his peak and to feel his body tense up and know that he was about to give me the nectar from his now, really hot and throbbing cock.

Though the emission in quantity is only between a tea and dessert spoon, it still seems to be a ladle full when it erupts and fills your mouth. It's only experience that stops you from gagging with the first copious jet that hits the roof of your palate and wants to slide down your throat. You hold it there in your mouth until he stops pumping his hips up to you and feel his body relax that you know that he's finished cumming. Then you can roll it round over the head of his cock before swallowing it and then licking him clean.

This release calmed Rosie down and he was then able to see to me in the same fashion. That we later then fucked each other goes without saying.

***

The days passed quickly and it was the start of our exams as it were, and though I seemed to have forgotten to say that when you do the breakfast shift, that's having to start at six in the morning, you do get to have three hours off during the afternoon.

So on the day that it was my turn to cook and serve up the four dinners for my exam, I was in a similar state as Rosie had been when he first saw his menu.

After we'd done our lunch time stint, we went up to our bedroom where we got undressed and went to bed together. Now it was his turn to calm me down and he made me forget the forthcoming dinner by getting me up on my knees and have him enter me from the rear, without a condom I might add.

It was lovely to feel his hard cock once again slide up into me, smoothing out the kinks in my canal, his hands stroking my waist and back as he slowly moved himself backwards and forwards, his hard shaft moving like a well-oiled piston. The gentle kiss of his thighs as they touched the cheeks of my bum as he did this until he got to the point of his coming. Then it was a smacking of our bodies as they clashed, feeling his balls bounce off me. His movements were faster and rougher as his fingers held my hips to pull me back onto him as he tried to get more of himself up inside me. Then came the lovely feel of his sperm shooting out to coat my insides as he held me tight as his hips kept pumping away.

My own cock would now be throbbing away and bouncing up and down, my balls swinging low below and me dribbling at the mouth as I had the pleasure of giving him pleasure at the same time as he fucked me.

But it's an experience and pleasure that doesn't last long and I gave out a cry as I felt him pull out, leaving that vacuum behind as the air seemed that much colder wafting round my ring piece as it began to shrink back in its closing.

I sighed in pleasure and fell onto my side as he left the bed to go and wash himself, a practice that was strictly adhered to when going bare back for the sake of hygiene. We had no worries about Aids for neither of us had been with another man in a sexual contact so we often had our anal sex without using condom.

With him now having washed himself, he got back onto the bed to receive a kiss and cuddle for a few minutes before it was my turn to get up behind him. His legs apart for me to get in between them and stroke the cheeks of his bum that my throbbing cock now wanted to penetrate.

With him lying forward on his forearms, his bum was high up and just at the right height for his ring piece to be level with my erection, which I guided to the orifice that was there in front of me. My left hand was on his hip as I held my cock in my right, guiding it to the right place.

Like me, his body flinched at the first touch of the head of my cock at his entrance and with just a slight pressure of my body, let go of my prick and placed that hand onto his other hip and slowly eased my body forward.

I could feel the resistance of his sphincter muscle as I kept up the pressure, watching the head of my cock get compressed slightly as it began to move into him and suddenly lose sight of it as it defeated his muscle and moved in, the shaft quickly following until it was out of sight and my thighs were tight up to the cheeks of his bum as his body heat now surrounded the whole length of my cock that was now buried inside him.

It's a similar pleasure you get in the giving as in the receiving as you slide back and forth in that tight aperture, crooning out words of love as you shaft and fuck the one you are giving the ultimate proof of this love. But it is still a short lived pleasure for it isn't long before nature takes over and you are soon thumping away at his rear as the sperm surges up from your swinging balls and erupts in that tight backside.

He too gave out a cry as I moved back and slid out of that hot interior of his body and got off the bed and went into the bathroom and carefully washed myself before returning to our bed for a kiss and cuddle from him. We did this along with much stroking of each other and fondling that which gives both of us pleasure till we were once more aroused for one of us to turn round and both take the head of the throbbing cock head into our mouths to suck and gently chew on while using the tongue to excite the erogenous G-spot area.

This form of sex can be prolonged more than fucking but the end result is the same, the coming of the body fluid to be savoured more by now being able to taste it before swallowing it and cleaning up the cock head.

I was much calmer now when we got up and had our shower before getting dressed and returning to the kitchen for me to prepare this meal for four. In this, you were allowed to have an assistant, this being Rosie, and so I cooked this meal that could possibly be the means of me getting a good position in some hotel or restaurant.

The soup off my menu, which I had to select, was a French onion soup. The entree would be a fillet of sole meunière with the main course being Duck à la orange, the vegetables chosen were mange-tout and new potatoes. For dessert I did a crème de menthe sorbet.

Rosie did the actual serving of each course as I was seeing to the next one and I'm sure that they were delighted in what I had cooked, well Rosie and I both enjoyed what I had cooked as we ate the same afterwards. We had a good drink in the bar afterwards before going to bed to hopefully celebrate a successful exam.

***

We then, well almost, did the same for Rosie when it was his turn to cook though it was more of a quickie for we only had an hour beforehand for his menu was for lunch. His menu was Vichyssoise soup, his choice followed by scallops in a cream sauce. Being really French, he picked Provençal chicken served up with French beans and duchess potatoes and finished with profiteroles with chocolate sauce.

Here, I assisted him and served up his cooked luncheon to the four teachers who would mark up his rating, though we couldn't celebrate with a drink till after dinner. But we had a good fucking session afterwards and as we lay there when finished, gently stroking each other's cock and balls did Rosie bring up the thoughts that had even run through my mind.

'Nicky,' he began after giving me a kiss. He now always called me Nicky when in bed ever since we had started fucking each other. 'Nicky. I'm going to miss this,' he said as he held my cock in his hand, slowly moving it as he gently squeezed it. I turned my face to him and saw that he had tears in his eyes. 'Also being in bed with you every night. Can't we somehow stay together?'

Our minds might have been on different tracks, but we were going in the same direction for I had had the same thought running through my mind.

'Rosie, Rosie, darling,' I said, my voice a little choked up with emotion at seeing those tears of his. 'I can't think of anywhere else I'd rather be than with you. I've not been looking forward to this course ending and..., and us having to part.' Holding his dick in my hand doing the same as he was doing to me. 'Have you any ideas, for I have?'

'Yes I have now, though I didn't really have any plans for the future when I first came here, except for doing well and then getting a job doing what I like doing. But since meeting you, I...I've found that I like doing what we have been doing together and want somehow for us to stay together. Do you want to stay with me? Really stay I mean?'

'Of course I do, my love,' I said, and meant it, in spite of seeing the anguish on his face and in his eyes. 'I do want us to stay together. Like us getting a flat or something and living together and finding a job where we can work together and spend every day, and night, with you,' I said, giving him a harder squeeze, my throat blocked with unshed tears and unable to say anymore, with my arm up under his neck as we cuddled together and almost cried. It was quite a few minutes before he could speak properly without choking.

'I said that I had an idea now and it was that we should try and stay working together and saving up enough money to be able to start a restaurant, the both of us.' I pushed away a lock of hair that had fallen across his face before giving him a kiss on the nose. His hair was now as long as mine for he'd stopped having his cut too and we both sported pony tails now, though for hygienic reasons, wore caps whilst in the kitchen or doing food preparation.

'That is a very good idea,' I said. 'I'm sure I could squeeze enough money out of dad for at least three months rent on a flat. Would you be able to get the same, though it wouldn't matter if you couldn't, for we would just have to find work quicker, that's all.'

'I don't think that'll be a problem though the flat would have to have two bedrooms. Just in case either of our parents paid us a visit for it would look strange to them if we only had the one bedroom.'

'Do you know, Rosie? I don't care now if my parents find out that I'll be living and sharing a bed with another man. My mother has asked if I'd made any girlfriends here at the college. I told her no, that I was too busy to make any attachments. But now, I just don't care if they find out that I love another man,' I said.

'Oh Nicky,' he said as he moved out of my arms and rolled over on top of me, his cock, which had now become aroused, getting squashed between our stomachs causing mine to rise up. 'I do love you too,' he cried, literally, for a few drops landed on my cheek before he kissed me quite passionately, which led on to his continuing his movement on top of me. This was in the mode of when we first went to bed together and I think we both enjoyed it, having our erections masturbated this way. We both cried with relief as we came, smearing our stomachs with the outpouring semen, which gave us an extra pleasure of then licking each other's stomach to remove the sticky mess we'd made.

'Tell you what,' I began after we had settled back down, an arm under each other's neck. 'We finish here next Friday and on the Saturday, that's what, three weeks away from now, it's my twenty-first birthday. Why don't you come and stay over at my place for the weekend and join in the celebration?' He gave out a chuckle.

'That's a good idea. That would make it, er, the 12th,' and gave out another chuckle. 'You can then come over to my house for mine, which is on the 26th, exactly two weeks later. We could then tell our parents exactly what we are planning.'

We then passionately kissed each other to seal the pact we had just made to be together in the future.

***

It was on the following Thursday evening that we all gathered together in the lounge and that included the first year students, to hear how the sophomores had got on with our exams. This was what we, Rosie and I, missed out the previous year for we had gone to bed early with it being our last night before the holiday. By the time Mr. Thompson, the senior teacher got his notes together, Rosie and I were sucking on each other's cocks, making pigs of ourselves in having this form of sex.

Mr. Thompson, flanked by the other three teachers, gave out a cough and called for our attention.

'We are pleased to announce that all of our second year students passed the exam with flying colours.' There were smiles all round amongst our twenty. 'But this year we do not have a clear winning student. Not two, but three of you received the same number of points,' and we all started to look at each other and all had looks of hope on their faces.

'With top score would have been one hundred and four which has never yet been attained, but this year, all three scored one hundred and one, which has never been attained since we opened this college. The others varying from one hundred down to eighty five which still earns them their diploma. But these have not yet been sorted out because we feel that it would be a letdown for that particular person to be credited with being at the tail end of this year's class.

'So will the three winners come forward and receive their diplomas first and for the rest of you, it will be in alphabetical order. So please, Nicholas Craig, Diane Lowe and Georges Roznoir, come forward.'

I'm sure my face was as red as both Diane's and Rosie's as our names had been read out, and now we went forward and shook hands with the teachers, getting their congratulations and we were handed our diplomas. There was much clapping of hands from all the others as we did so and went back into the crowd as it were, as the others all received theirs too.

Us second year students then got a free drink at the bar where Rosie and I both opted to have a vodka and tonic, which became our usual tipple later. The bar also stayed open till eleven that night, to which we stayed until it closed before saying our goodnights and going up to our room.

In the bedroom, we went and stood under the now sorry looking sprig of mistletoe and kissed each other in the joy of both of us coming on top.

'I think,' said Rosie, looking up as we still had our arms around each other, 'That the mistletoe there has brought, not only us together, but brought us luck at the same time. I'm never going to forget this.'

'Neither am I,' I replied. 'I'm glad that I went and hung it there, and that's where it's staying and I hope it brings the next occupants the same luck that it has given us.'

'Do you think that they will fall in love too?' Rosie asked.

'I don't think lightning strikes twice in the same place, but they will be damned lucky if it happens,' I said, pulling Rosie close again to kiss. It was with undue haste that we quickly took our clothes off, throwing them in the direction of our chairs, both of us sporting fine looking erections.

'God I love this,' said Rosie as he went down onto his knees in front of me, holding my erection and taking the head into his opening mouth, his tongue pushing the foreskin right back. I gave out a groan as his lips closed round it and felt his tongue weaving across the bare flesh as my hands gently rested on his bobbing head.

'Not too much Rosie for I'd rather fuck you with it,' I gasped.

'I want you to too,' he said releasing me and it almost looked as if the head of my cock was steaming. 'And without a condom,' he said as he quickly got onto the bed on his knees, leaning forward so that his backside was high up. We didn't need any cream for the head was coated in his saliva and it bobbed about as I got onto the bed behind him. In between his knees, I stroked the cheeks of his bum first before bending my head down and giving each one a kiss before straightening up and placing the head of my really throbbing cock to his back passage entrance.

What a lovely sensation it is to see and feel the head of your cock slowly disappear into the tightness of his backside and feel the heat from his body as well as the muscle there, flexing away as the shaft filled him too. With my thighs up tight to the cheeks of his bum, I gave my cock a twitch to make him give out a groan and also made him gasp and give out a shiver as I ran my fingernails up and down the sides of his chest.

Then holding his hips loosely with my hands, I began to move myself in and out of that tight passage, loving the thrill of having a glorious fuck of the man I was now really in love with. I didn't last long and was soon holding his hips tighter as I pulled him backwards to my forward thrusts, grunting now as I forcefully rammed myself up into him, my swinging balls slapping against his lower bum cheeks. It was with more grunts and heaves. Almost lifting him up from the bed as I held him tight as my hips pumped away, letting my seed shoot out into his lovely backside.

'Oh God I love this when I feel you come inside me,' he gasped as I slowly came to a stop, panting heavily, now leaning over his rear end. 'If only it could last longer.'

'We'll see if you can go longer,' I said as I began to pull out of him.

'Noooo!' He cried at my withdrawal, knowing the sensation he was getting at feeling it being removed from his backside, but it came free and bounced about as I got off the bed and staggered through to the bathroom to wash myself.

He was lying there on his back when I returned, his full erection lying there up on his stomach and I watched it twitch as I got back onto the bed.

'This is a lovely cock that you've got,' I said as I lifted it up and opened my mouth as I bent my head and took the head of it into my mouth and did the same to him as he had done to me. Pushing the foreskin back down so that I could tease him with both tongue and teeth, also coating it with saliva. God, I loved his cock and couldn't wait to have it pushed up into me and so quickly released him and moved over and up onto my knees in the same position to receive that wonderful tool that he had.

What a thrill it gave me to feel the head slowly enlarging the entrance to my canal and then have the soothing massage as he slid fully inside my backside, trying to give him pleasure by using my sphincter muscle flexing it as he entered me.

I was in heaven at feeling his hands holding my hips as his cock moved back and forth inside me, making me gurgle with delight and hoping against hope that he would indeed last longer than me in this fucking mode. But he didn't, for he was soon tightening his grip as he began to reach his peak, thrusting away as hard as he could, trying to get more of himself inside me and gave me the joy of feeling his sperm splash the insides, making me drool at the pleasure I was getting from his fucking of me.

I also loved having his weight bearing down on my lower back as he panted, feeling his cock still twitching away inside me, but I also cried out when he started to pull out. What an incredible feeling of loss that runs through the body at the feel of that wonderful tool of pleasure being removed making one cry out. That is the worse part of this sexual act, the removal of the toy if I can call it that, feeling like a small boy that's been deprived of his favourite plaything.

But one still holds that wonderful glow in one's belly and heart from the pleasure that has been given to you. So it was with open arms that I welcomed him back onto the bed when he returned from washing his prick, now looking on the limp side as it swung about as he came into my arms for a kiss.

We later went down on each other to suck and chew on our respective cock heads and even later, fucked one another again and it must have been well after four in the morning before we fell asleep, both sucking on each other like babies with dummies in their mouths.

Both bleary-eyed in the morning, trying to revive ourselves under the shower before getting dressed to help in the kitchen after breakfast to prepare our last lunch at the college for we would be leaving just after this.

It didn't take long to pack our few things away and spent longer in saying our goodbye to each other under the mistletoe. We'd already noted each other's phone number and I promised to ring and tell him when to arrive at my home for my birthday party the following day.

We said our goodbyes to the teachers and thanked them and so, with our diplomas safely tucked away in out suitcases, we left Derwent College for the last time to go home, looking forward to a good future.

***

Mum and dad were at home when I arrived, their school year having just finished too. They were over the moon when I told them I came on top of the class, along with two others, in our year and this pleased them no end and thought that the cost of the past two years well worth it. Along with the diploma there was a letter that roughly said that I showed enormous talent and flair for cooking and achieving one of the highest points in my subsequent examination, which would be good as a reference as one could get for obtaining a job.

Mum insisted that she cook dinner that night and so it was a change that I could relax. It was over dinner that I was asked the question of where I think I would be applying for a job. Now Rosie and I had discussed this in depth and it was what we had come up with that I now told my parents.

I told them more in depth of the person I had shared a room with at the college, calling Rosie by his proper name, Georges, saying that he was half French and that his surname was Roznoir, which mother picked up on straight away.

'Roznoir! Rose black, the black rose,' she said, turning to dad for his benefit.

'Yes. That's as far as his family could trace him back. To Agincourt where he was a knight with that on his shield,' I told them. 'Well, he and I would like to stay and work together but to start with an agency rather than tie ourselves to one particular hotel or restaurant. It would give us time to see exactly how hotel kitchens were run before making any final decision. It would mean us moving closer into London to be able to get to any hotel or other place in quick time to act as a replacement or something along those lines.'

'Aiming higher than a hotel or restaurant here in Harrow then?' my dad asked, in not a really well concealed touch of sarcasm.

'With all due respect to what there is in Harrow, I know that I can prepare meals better than what they offer. Yes, I am aiming higher but not as high as the Ritz or Savoy as yet, but have other ideas along with Ro....Georges. We want to work together and save up enough to start our own restaurant, somewhere in London where the money is. We're both good chefs and just know that we would make a success of it.'

I flopped back in my chair having said my piece and waited for the inevitable come-backs, which didn't take long to come, mostly from my dad. These I fielded as best I could and waited until he'd come to a halt.

'Look! It's my twenty-first in two weeks time and I have invited Georges to come and celebrate with us and I'll get him to see to our Sunday dinner and you can then see that he is as good as I am in this line of work.'

There was more but I waited until I knew that mum was on my side before bringing up the subject of being lent enough money to be able to pay three months rent on a flat somewhere in South London.

'Okay,' from dad. 'When you've paid back the loan for this rent, how will you save enough for a restaurant?' was his reply

'Well it's obvious that we will eat where we work and then only have to pay the rent and electricity. We will survive and will save the wages paid to us, that I can assure you,' I said, and then the subject was dropped and not brought up again until Rosie was with us.

The fortnight flew by and a table had been reserved at the best restaurant that Harrow could provide and I'd already phoned Rosie and agreed to meet him at Harrow station on the Friday afternoon.

I was there on time and didn't mind that he was fifteen minutes late for it's difficult to be precise with the underground's timetables. We both smiled as he came through and I could see in his eyes that he would have liked to kiss me as much as I had wanted to, but we settled for a hug in our greeting. There were always two taxis waiting outside of the station and so it wasn't long before we were at my home and led him inside.

'Mum, dad, meet Georges, my roommate at the college.'

'Welcome to our home, Georges,' mum said and was flattered when he took her hand and kissed it in the Gaelic fashion and thanked her for the welcome in French. I'd already told him that she was a French teacher at her school as well as being French herself, and I saw that it went down rather well and that drew her closer to my side in the argument about me moving into a flat with him. He shook dad's hand and thanked him in English before I said that I would show him where his room was. This I did and couldn't wait until we were inside.

'This is the welcome I wanted to give you at the station,' I said as I took him into my arms and we kissed. Rather a long one and it nearly drove me mad for I wanted to there and then, strip off his clothes and have sex, but held back. I showed him where the bathroom and toilet were and which was my room, but whispered that it would be in his that I would spend the nights.

Mum helped me prepare the dinner for that evening, leaving Rosie alone with dad for him to question Rosie about that I had stated about our future. Mum was now definitely on my side and it was up to Rosie to get dad in coming over as it were. This wasn't apparent until the following day.

Dinner was great that evening and it wasn't long before Rosie tried to hide a fake yawn that I jumped in and apologised for talking too much and said that it was time for bed. We said our goodnights and upstairs, I whispered to Rosie that I would have to wait until my parents had settled down before going to his room which he accepted.

It was close to an hour before I could slip out of bed and put on a dressing gown and go along to where Rosie was. He was awake and threw back the bed covers as I dropped my dressing gown and got into bed and into his arms for a welcome kiss.

Boy, did we suck and fuck that night? Not half, and I didn't dare go to sleep in his bed as it was close to three o'clock and it wouldn't look good if I was seen in the morning, coming out of his room, so at least I got a few hours sleep in my own room.

'Many Happy Returns of the Day!' was the greeting I got from the three when I turned up downstairs in the morning for it was now the 12th of August. I sat down for breakfast and opened my cards and thanked them and it was with a shy smile that Rosie pushed a small wrapped gift across to me. I opened it and saw that he had given me a lovely silver bracelet with Nicky inscribed on it, the name we only used in bed when we were together. I thanked him and then noticed that it was also inscribed on the inside which I didn't show my parents for it read, With love, Rosie.

I would have loved to have kissed him, but patted his hand instead as I thanked him. I then looked expectantly at mum and dad, waiting to see what they had bought me for my birthday. Dad gave a little cough and then passed across to me, an envelope.

'Your mother and I spoke last night and having now met Georges, thought that this would suffice as your birthday present.'

I looked at mum who nodded with a big smile on her face as I then opened the envelope and took out a cheque and gasped, for it was made out to me for five thousand pounds. I jumped up as I passed cheque across to Rosie and gave first mum a kiss and then dad in the Gaelic fashion where both cheeks are kissed.

Rosie was all smiles as he handed the cheque back to me, now knowing that I got half of the rent money and it was now up to him to get the other half.

It was a gay day and the dinner that night was good though both of us knew that we could turn out a better meal, but as we hadn't had to cook it, it passed muster. It was good that we had taken a taxi there for we were quite in our cups when it was time to leave having consumed quite a bit of alcohol. It didn't stop me from later going off to Rosie's room for him to give me another present and had to laugh when he pulled the covers off of himself to find that he'd tied a big red ribbon round the base of his erection. I loved both the thought and his cock which he then served up to me and I thoroughly enjoyed being given this big present.

I only stayed there long enough to give him the same back, loving to fuck this love of mine in my own home and couldn't really wait until we had a place of our own to make love whenever we felt like it.

Rosie showed his expertise in giving us a lovely lunch the following day, it being Sunday and thanked him for being a proper gentleman while in my home and we again fucked each other with me not leaving his room until the early hours of the morning.

He thanked mum and dad the following morning and said that he had never had such a lovely weekend and I saw him off at the station and promised to be at his home in a fortnight's time.

***

When it came round, it was almost a replica of the time he stayed at my home, convincing his father about how we would work together and achieve our aim of getting our own restaurant. I said replica because I too passed across a gift that was a silver bracelet too with Georges inscribed on the outside and Love from Nicky on the inside. With him telling his parents of how I had received a cheque for five thousand pounds as my birthday gift, he too received the same as he was wished a Happy Birthday.

I think it's pointless for me to say that it was him that came to my room on those three nights for us to make love to each other in the only way two males can, by sucking each other's organ before having said organ thrust up into our back passage to give us both the thrill in the giving and receiving of such a wonderful weapon.

Farewells were said on the Monday morning but instead of him seeing me off at the station, he joined me as we now were out hunting for a flat that we would call our home to live, sleep and make love in.

We left our suitcases in luggage lockers at Waterloo station and went flat hunting without seeing one that we liked on that first day. So we spent the night in a small hotel that wasn't very good but at least it had a bed to which we fell into and spent our first night away from anybody else and made pigs of ourselves in having sex both in the bed, on the floor and even having each other next morning in the bath.

We had to have a place quite close to the station for us to get around or across London quite quickly and it wasn't until the afternoon and with a different estate agent, found one that suited us in both location, size and rental costs.

It was a two-bedroom flat, furnished and ready for occupancy and so we agreed, and back at the agency, signed the agreement form and paid three months rent in advance and moved in that evening. It was by then getting late and so we went and bought a Chinese takeaway and ate our first meal in our new home, together.

Though it had two bedrooms, we would only be using one of them unless we had visitors and then we would have to make the other look as though it was in use. So it was into what would be our room and it was almost a tease parade as we slowly undressed as if to show our flesh to each other for the first time.

He thought it amusing when I turned him around and went down on my knees and kissed both cheeks of his bum but not when I went and stuck a finger up his arse. That made him jump and quickly turn around, which was what I wanted for I now had his erection in front of my eyes and just ready for me to take into my mouth, which I did and got a big sigh from him.

'Not too much, Nicky,' he said. 'Let's put it where it likes to go.' Well it was where I wanted it to go too, so I let his throbbing cock slip out of my mouth and quickly got onto the bed, unmade as yet, and went up onto my knees as I felt him get on the bed behind me.

Oh what bliss it was to feel his cock head touch my entrance before he pushed his way inside me. Having it once again, pulsating inside as he soothed and smoothed the wrinkles out of, not only the canal, but my mind as well. I loved this man behind me, who gave me the thrill of his moving hard piece of flesh as he fucked me till he came, filling my backside with his semen.

I gave out the usual cry at the loss I felt with him pulling out to go and wash himself for we hadn't even stopped unpacking our suitcases to find the condoms there.

He gave me a kiss on the lips first before moving down and taking the head of my now really paining cock head, into his mouth to give me some sucks and also to help in the lubrication before letting me go and assuming the right position for me to now fuck him.

How lovely to feel the inner heat of his body as my cock slid into his backside, having it compressed to feel it being gripped all around as I slowly began to move myself in our fucking mode. But this time, I leaned heavily on his rear end and made him collapse onto the bed so that I could lay my full weight on his back. He gave out a grunt as I landed on him and got my hands up under his armpits to grasp his shoulders and this was to give me grip as I began to ram myself up into him. God it was lovely to hear him grunting at every forward push into him and then to get his squeals of delight as he felt my sperm shoot up into him.

We lay joined together like this for several minutes with us trying to get more breath back into our bodies, both of us sweating with the exertions and made him cry out as he felt me pulling myself out of his backside.

Instead of using the wash basin, after staggering to the bathroom, I got into the shower and washed myself there and he had to wait until I'd finished before he could have a shower too. Dried, but still naked, I went out of the bathroom and looked in various cupboards until I found the bed linen and took this back to the bedroom as he came out from his shower. On seeing me still naked, stayed the same and between us, made up the bed properly before emptying our suitcases and putting the things away before getting into the bed proper to kiss and cuddle before falling asleep.

***

We were hungry when we woke up and it wasn't for sex but food. A Chinese meal is filling but it doesn't really last and as we hadn't as yet laid out any supplies, we quickly did our morning things before getting dressed and going out to find a cafe of sorts for us to have breakfast. This we did not far from Waterloo station, after which, we found a small supermarket and bought enough food for a few days, well all that we could carry in their plastic bags without them splitting. We also bought a local newspaper which we devoured in looking at the job vacancies in the area. But there was nothing of note or worthy of our talents, besides, we still had to register at a job centre to get our National Insurance Number.

It was in the afternoon that we found the local one and after an hour or so, we both had our numbers, having carried our birth certificates with us and gave the flat as our address. We also got addresses of some catering agencies for this was what we had decided to do to start with.

We thought it prudent to start with an agency so that we could, hopefully, get to work together in a few different hotels and restaurants to see just how things went on in these places rather than jump into a full time job and then hate the place. Mind you, we both could have gotten jobs straight away from the Job Centre, but this was the way we were going to try first.

We spent the following morning at an Internet café and spoke to several agencies before we made a move for we had enough money for another three months rent and food too for this period, but to cut to the chase as it were, we finally got accepted at one such agency that was quite pleased at seeing that we had just come from Derwent College and having been shown our letters and diplomas.

The only drawback to this was that it was unlikely for us to both get work at the same place at the same time, except when there was a special party being laid on and the agency was asked to do the catering. But it was all a learning curve and it was an eye opener as regarding the different setups each place had, the hotels being the worse in their pecking order in the kitchens. Also the manner of speaking like when you spoke to the chef or answer him, it had to be "Yes, chef," "No, chef." We were also looked upon as being interlopers even though we were only there to help them when they were short-handed. The restaurants were better and it wasn't long before we began to get asked for by name at the agency which boosted our spirits up, but it took a few months before that started to happen.

At wherever we worked, it would usually be for a week or two for other staff to have their holiday or someone had gone off sick. If we both got jobs at hotels, we would normally finish around the same time and get home at the same time. If a restaurant, we could be working later in the evening, but we did learn an awful lot with this moving around.

There were some days and nights that we didn't have to work and on these, we would quite often go out and have some drinks at either a club or bar which gave us another insight as to how they worked their staff.

While working, our sex life was somewhat curtailed, especially when we finished at different hours, but it didn't diminish our love for each other and we always made up for lost time when we weren't working.

We also found that there were many men like us in this industry, those who would rather have sex with another male than a woman. We both got hit on at various jobs with the usual approach, like are you married, have you got a girlfriend? I made no bones about that I was living with another male which led them to ask at how long I've been with my partner. It appeared that when saying over two years now, it would lead to the question if I would like to have a change?

This was in a restaurant called Cavalleros and it then clicked as to what this place was about for it seemed to be always populated by male couples. The name was a joke for in the Spanish language, a B is almost the same sounding as a V and the word caballero in English is gentleman. It was a restaurant for gays, which I should now really say that both Rosie and myself were of this ilk as we had male sex together.

Anyway, this other cook, for that is what he was for he was nowhere near being able to be called a chef, came on to me. Saying that I looked like a strong man and he would like to see if I was big in the right department and eventually got around to saying that he would like to suck on my cock. This was during the afternoon when the place was closed and we were preparing food for the evening dinners when I eventually said yes. We went into the storeroom and there I leaned up against the door and he had a big smile on his face as I pulled my erection out of my trousers and his smile got bigger as he saw it, and licking his lips, went down onto his knees and took me into his mouth.

Christ, I learned then how to really give head for he was doing a better job on me than Rosie had ever done and I gave out a loving groan as his tongue and teeth teased the bare flesh of my cock as his head went back and forth on me. Such was his expertise in this that I was soon holding his head between my hands as I face fucked him, coming with quite some vigour.

His eyes were twinkling as he looked up at me as I finished coming and could see him then swallowing my outburst before he then sucked and licked me clean.

'That was just lovely, Nick,' he said as he sat back on his heels, licking his lips again. 'Can I say thank you with a kiss?' he asked as he rose up as I put my now deflating cock away.

'I can only say yes, Stephen, for that was bloody good,' I replied, letting him move into my arms for the kiss. And so for the two weeks that I worked there, he went down on me every afternoon. I didn't tell Rosie that I had let Stephen suck on me.

Rosie too was being hit upon by the chef that he was working with in the Pendant Hotel where he was currently working. This he told me in bed the second night after he had started there. We had just been down on each other and he was pleased in the way that I had sucked and chewed on him.

'The chef at the hotel, he lives in, wants me to fuck him,' Rosie said as he stroked my chest.

'Well fuck him then,' I said. This made him sit up and look down at me.

'You'll let me do this? Fuck another man?' he asked somewhat astounded that I would say that he could.

'Yes,' I said as I pulled his head down and kissed him. 'As long as you don't fall in love with him and use a condom.'

'Fall in love with him? He's old enough to be my father. You... you wouldn't mind then?'

'No, as long as you use a condom and come back to me,' I said, giving him another kiss, 'For I love you so much that I say yes so that you'll appreciate what we both have now.'

'Oh Nicky,' he said, tears coming to his eyes. 'I do really, really love you and I could not love any other man as I do you,' he said, the tears now running down his face and leaned over and kissed me with quite some passion which raised me up to a full erection. 'Make love to me, Nicky. Fuck me without a rubber, for I like to feel you coming inside me.'

This I then proceeded to do with him up on his knees and me behind him, loving the tightness of his backside as I moved my cock back and forth inside him with his muscle flexing away as I shafted him. We both crooned at the massage I was giving to his insides while he was giving me the pleasure of fucking the man I loved.

Mind you, I got as much pleasure when he was behind me with his prick doing the same to me and cried out when I felt his semen splash my insides as he came to much grunting on his part as he tried to stuff as much of himself into me at the same time.

So the next day he went and fucked his chef while I was having my cock sucked at my work place. Rosie was home in bed before me and he quickly kissed me all over telling me that the chef was nothing like being in bed with me, crying as he said this.

'Though I enjoyed fucking him, I was thinking and wishing that it was you beneath my hands.' So I went beneath him once again for him to give us both pleasure in his fucking of me. It was when I was up behind and inside him that he spoke which gave me food for thought.

'Oh Nicky, darling,' he gasped as I moved inside him. 'I do like being the female for you.'

This reminded me of the pleasure I had got when I had put on my mother's underwear, the thrill of feeling the lace bra and the erotic sensations I got when I pulled on her nylon stockings to fix them to the belt. Christ, didn't I ram myself into him then with these memories running through my mind. What would Rosie think if he saw me dressed up in this fetish underwear? Would it turn him on as much as it did to me? Well there was only one way of finding out, but left it until we both finished our stints at the present jobs and before the next one.

I went out and into a department store and bought a complete set of lingerie and to top this off, I even bought a dress though I had to guess the size, and a pair of low heeled shoes to finish off the ensemble. I wouldn't let him see what I had bought when I got back to the flat and got him to go out to the shops to get some special delicacies for dinner that evening. This would give me enough time to surprise him when he returned.

I had a quick shower and laid out what I had bought on the bed and sat down and pulled on the stockings first. Boy, didn't my cock rise up as the nylon whispered up my legs as I pulled them up before putting on the belt and standing up to fix the tops into the studs. Next came the bra which I had to fix from the front before twisting it round and putting my arms through the straps and fit them snugly over my shoulders. I used a pair of socks to pad out the cups and I knew that it looked good when I stood up and looked at myself in the dressing table mirror.

I'd guessed the size of the dress correctly and it fitted nicely to my body after I had pulled it down over my head and hips, loving the feel as I smoothed down the sides. Next to see to was my hair which now hung down to just over my shoulders when I'd released it from the band that held it up in the fashion of a pony tail. I sat down at the dressing table that we had in our bedroom and brushed my hair forward to come from the back to fall down both sides of my face. It just reached my shoulders now and even without further brushing, it looked just right and looking at myself in the mirror, wondered what I would really look like if I used some cosmetics, like kohl on the eyelids and a light dusting of face powder. A light shade of lipstick would go well and tried to imagine at how it would change my looks.

But as I didn't have any cosmetics, I shelved the idea for I wanted to see Rosie's reaction to seeing me dressed in this feminine way first. If he liked it, maybe we could take this a bit further in more ways than one. Satisfied as to how I looked, I stood up and automatically ran my hands down the sides of the dress to smooth it so no wrinkles showed and felt myself getting an erection with this simple action and had to really try and control this as I went out into our sitting room to wait for Rosie to come home, which wasn't long.

'It's me, Nicky,' he called out as he entered the front door. 'I've got all that we wanted,' he spoke as he came into the room and his face was a picture when he saw me standing there, dressed as I was.

'Oh my God!' he exclaimed, dropping the two bags of shopping and putting his hand up to his mouth. 'Nicky, darling! You look absolutely stunning!' he said, moving towards me. I now had a big smile on my face as he came into my open arms and gave me a lovely big kiss, pulling me tight to his body for me to feel the erection that he had suddenly acquired at seeing me like this. 'I just can't believe how gorgeous you look,' he exclaimed after breaking off the kiss and standing back to run his eyes up and down my body, still holding my arms.

'You like it?' I asked, breaking away from him and doing a quick spin round, making the dress flare out as I did so.

'Oh yes,' he breathed out, his eyes wide and shining. 'Oh yes.'

'Well, wait until you see what's underneath,' I said, still with this smile on my face at seeing his facial expression when he first saw me.

'I know what's underneath,' he said with him still smiling.

'Apart from that,' I replied, knowing he was only referring to my body as I slipped the tops of the dress off my shoulders for it to slither down to the floor. His face was another picture and I wished I'd had a camera to catch his wide eyed expression as he saw the underwear.

'Oh my God,' he repeated, his voice a little hoarse as his eyes took in the padded bra, the brief panties that were restraining the erection inside, the suspender belt hold up the black stockings that I don't think he'd noticed earlier.

'Oh Nicky, how wonderful you look,' he said as he started to unzip his trousers and pulled out his erect and throbbing cock. 'I want you so much,' his voice tight and quavering as he moved towards me, his cock sticking out in front and I wanted what I could see too. I turned round and bent over the back of the armchair, feeling the side straps of the suspender belt sliding around my thighs as I did so. I knew that he liked the sight of the tight cheeks of my bum as he came behind me and stroked them as well as running his hand over the suspender straps and the tops of my stockings before pulling the panties aside.

The head of his cock pushed in between the cheeks and I felt him start to enlarge the entrance to my backside and I began to drool as I felt him enter me, filling that vacant slot with his lovely hard tool. The soothing massage as he filled my channel until his trousered thighs came up to the bare cheeks of my bum.

'Oh Nicky,' he groaned, leaning over my rear end to run his hands up and down the sides of my chest before starting to move his throbbing erection inside me. Such was his ardour that it wasn't long after he moved in and out of me when he held me tight and began to pump his seed up into me

'Darling, darling, my darling,' he crooned as he jerked off inside me, panting heavily as he finally came to a halt, his cock still throbbing away inside. I couldn't help give out that little cry as I felt him pulling out and heard him move out of the sitting room to go and wash himself for having had me bareback. I now groaned at the loss as I felt my ring piece puckering back to close up as I straightened up and turned round and pulled my own erection out of the top of the panties as he came back with his cock now back inside his trousers. I leaned back against the armchair, holding my erection out for him to see.

He smiled as he came towards me, licking his lips as he went down onto his knees before me and took my cock into his hand as I released it and took the head into his open mouth. He was getting better and better at this cock-sucking as I gave out a groan at feeling his tongue and teeth attack the G-spot and it wasn't long before I was holding his head in my hands as I face fucked him, shooting out quite a quantity of sperm for him to swallow. He squeezed and sucked out what little remained inside before licking the exposed head clean before standing up and taking me into his arms for a long and amorous kiss.

'Nicky, darling. That was a wonderful surprise,' he said when we broke apart. 'Do you have anymore?'

'Just one darling,' I said.

'What's that?' he asked, his eyes alight again.

'I want you to see the expression on my face when I can see you wearing these things,' I said with a smile upon seeing his face. 'After dinner, you can put them on and I can then make love to you acting the part of the female. But as I'm almost naked now,' I carried on as I pushed my now deflating cock back inside the panties, 'You can get your clothes off and help me get dinner.'

He quickly undressed and we took the two bags of groceries into the small kitchen where I got out a small pinny for him as I didn't want his front to get splashed, tying the ribbons at the back, stroking the cheeks of his bare bum as I did so.

It didn't take long for us to prepare the meal and it was soon eaten and when the things were all washed up and put away, it was time for him to get dressed. With his pinny coming off, he was obviously looking forward to this for he already had a massive erection that I longed to touch and stroke but held myself back.

We went into our bedroom where I, with some loathing, took off my female garb and then lay down naked on the bed to watch him put on these things. I nearly laughed at him trying to attach the hooks of the suspender belt with them being behind his back and had to tell him to do it from the front first before turning it round. He didn't need to be told a second time when it came to putting on the bra. It was fun to see him struggling to get the studs of the suspender straps to fit properly when he'd pulled up the stockings. He tried to wear the panties but gave up as he couldn't fit his erection inside them, the head sticking out of the top. Putting on the dress was easy enough and he finally sat down at the dressing table and released his hair from the pony tail. His hair was as long as mine and he brushed it forward as I had done and he looked lovely when it was down, framing his face and tried to picture him with make-up on too. For when he stood up and turned around to me, it was as if I was really looking at a woman dressed before me.

'Well?' He asked as his hands smoothed the sides of the dress and the only incongruity was his erection pushing out the front.

'Perfect. Just perfect,' I said in awe, seeing that he actually looked better than I did in a dress and decided that I should get him one, plus the underwear so that we could both be dressed at the same and have fun at acting the part of a woman. He gave a pout when I told him to take the dress off but did so smiling for he could see that my cock was up and hard ready to fuck him. He wanted me too for he pulled it off quicker than he'd put it on and he looked gorgeous in just the underwear when it was revealed. Onto the bed he came and into my arms for a kiss and it felt strange to feel the two lumps of the bra up against my chest as we kissed, him lying half on top of me. But with two throbbing cocks getting squashed, we didn't want to lose the pleasure of the fuck we were about to have, so he soon moved off for me to rise up onto my knees and shuffle behind him as he assumed the normal position for our lovemaking.

I drooled at the sight before me as I moved in between his open legs. The suspender belt around his waist and the straps down by the side of his thighs holding up the tops of the stockings, and with the strap of the bra across his back really gave the impression that it was a woman kneeling there in front of me. The only difference is that I could only see the entrance to his backside between the cheeks of his bum and not the aperture of a female below it.

But a hole is a hole and I believed that his would be tighter than the right place of a woman, not yet having had the experience of fucking a woman. But with Rosie here looking just like a female, I didn't need or really have the desire of having one.

I wasn't wearing a condom and just loved to see the head of my erection pushing slowly up into him, seeing it getting compressed as it moved in and loving the feel of the heat of his inner body as I moved even further inside until my thighs were hard up against the cheeks of his bum.

We both let out a sigh when I was fully inside and could feel his muscle constantly squeezing me and holding his hips firmly, began to move myself in the process of fucking this man that I now really loved. He gave out a shiver when I raked my fingernails down the sides of his chest and gave out a low moan and began to move his body back onto me. It was a lovely fuck, holding him tight as I came, sending my seed deep up into him as he gave out little cries at feeling it hit his insides.

He gave out another cry when I pulled out and got off the bed to go and wash myself and upon my return, saw him lying on his back with a big smile on his face and having an erection himself now.

'That was a lovely fuck, Nicky, and I'm up and ready to give the same again to you,' he said, stroking himself before moving his hand up and running his hand over a cup of the bra he was wearing. 'And I got a lovely feeling inside me when I put these things on.'

'Would you like us to go and buy you some?' I asked as I got onto the bed, with him moving up onto his knees, his cock waving about as he did so.

'Oooh yes, Nicky, darling. We can then be two girls together,' he said with a girlish giggle as I leaned forward and gave the head of his cock a suck to give it some lubrication.

'Okay,' I said, letting go of him and turning around on the bed. 'We'll go out after breakfast and get some for you.'

So I had my girlfriend Rosie fuck me again and with him being so big and hard, it was pure joy having him back inside me after so short a time when he last fucked me.

***

He said that he had hated taking those female things off as we got dressed into our male clothes after breakfast and was eager for us to go out and buy him a set. This we did and didn't care what the shop assistant thought as I made sure that the bra we bought would fit him. So with his lingerie bought, we also went into a beauty parlour where I bought a cosmetic case with all the creams, powder and make-up inside before we returned home.

It was good that we hadn't been called by the agency with a job or two for we both had fun getting dressed up as two girls, both of us getting erections as we pulled on our stockings and as we fitted the strap studs into the tops of the stockings. From behind, wearing the underwear and our hair down, we really did look like females and it look so incongruous when seen from the front with our erections standing out proud. They clashed together when we kissed and both of us were hungry for them to be used in our normal fashion.

It was a glorious session we both had, fucking the girl that we had dressed up to be. After which, we played about with the cosmetics in trying to make our faces look like real women. Mind you, it took quite a good few days and goes at doing this before we could put the stuff on properly and it was several weeks before we were brave enough to actually leave the flat wearing these clothes out in the open.

What a thrill that gave us, walking down the street as women and trying to emulate the way that they walked. Though bearing in mind when we had gotten dressed for this parade that we wore tight underpants to prevent our erections poking out the front of our dresses.

***

In between this, we both had various jobs from the agency and we were now beginning to be asked for by name, which means our cooking abilities were now being recognised. Most times we worked at a place for at least a week if not a fortnight while the person we were replacing was on holiday so we didn't do many one-night stands for when a chef was off sick.

Rosie got his end away with the head chef again at the hotel he was working at, and even with my permission, let himself be fucked by the chef during the afternoon break. I, at the same time, was back at the Cavalleros where instead of Stephen just sucking on me, we finished up fucking each other and he wasn't bad but not as good as Rosie when he used his cock up behind me.

It was through him that I learned of a gay bar not far from where we lived and so Rosie and I began to go there on a regular basis when we had some nights off. We were surprised at how many couples, all men, went there, and got on quite well with them, all knowing that they fucked their partners. As Rosie and I now had sex with other men at various times at work, we thought it's a good idea to have another male or two spend the night at our place, just for us to have a full night of sex with another man so that we could appreciate each other even more.

There was one couple in the bar that we got on very well with, drinking and talking, and found out that they quite often swapped partners. So one night, we asked if they would like to come to our place for dinner, and stay if they wanted to. They agreed to this and so set it up for the following evening where we would meet in the bar early for a drink before going to our place.

We made sure the flat was clean and tidy and had laid in the makings for a good meal before we went off to meet them. They were Robin and Andrew, though they called each other by their female names when alone at their home, they went by Robina and Andria.

I think that all four of us were excited when we met in the bar and only stayed for one drink before leaving for our place. It wasn't that far for us to walk and were quite pleased with the pad we had and said so as we opened some bottles of wine to drink as Rosie and I began preparing our dinner.

Both Robin and Andrew couldn't praise our cooking enough when we'd finished eating everything we'd cooked. Both saying that we would do well at any high class hotel or restaurant for they couldn't fault the presentation or taste of the four courses we produced. We had gone through four bottles of wine and it was when we were having coffee and brandy afterwards in the sitting room that the subject of our sleeping arrangements were brought up.

It was shyly asked, by Andrew I think, on who would be sleeping with whom. It had already been decided between Rosie and myself that he would be using the spare bedroom this night and as I finished my brandy, stood up and held out my hand to Andrew.

'Time for bed,' I said and saw that with my hand out to him that he blushed and took it as he stood up. I saw the smiles on the faces of Rosie and Robin as they too got up and followed Andrew and me to our bedrooms.

It seemed strange to see another person undress in my bedroom, to have this other naked man before me, having an erection the same as mine and also see that he wasn't quite as big as Rosie. But an erect cock will give the same pleasure regardless of the size and length of it, for it would still seem to be the right size when inside.

'Kiss me, Andrew,' I said as we moved towards each other.

'In a bedroom, my name is Andria,' he said shyly, his eyes sparkling, which I believe was in seeing the size of my organ that he would soon be having. We came close together in an embrace and kissed, our cocks clashing as they were pressed up between us.

His kissing technique was different to Rosie's as I'm sure mine was to him, but it was still another thrill just to be kissing someone else in my own room.

We broke off the kissing and got onto the bed where alongside, were several packets of condoms as well as a pot of cream, but as I got a condom out for me to wear he wanted to give my cock a suck first before I fucked him. This he did, taking the head into his mouth and worked his tongue round it very well indeed, using his teeth too to rasp the swollen head before letting it go, a big smile on his face.

I rolled the condom down on myself and he said that he didn't need the cream as he got onto his knees, presenting me with the view of his rear end which wasn't unlike that of Rosie's.

I felt him give out a shiver when he felt the head of my cock touch the aperture it was going to go into, and holding his hips firm, I leaned in and felt his sphincter muscle automatically trying to prevent the entry, but failed, and I soon slid myself up into his backside.

There was an explosion of breath from him when I was fully inside and tight up to the cheeks of his bum, having held his breath the whole time that I was slowly pushing myself up into him.

'God that's big,' he breathed out with the gasp, his muscle flexing itself round the shaft, and I then began to move, trying to give him the best fuck that I could. I think he liked it for he was softly crooning as I held him tighter to myself as I came inside him, jerking away with my hips until I had given out all that I had there in my balls at the time. I even evinced a cry from him as I pulled back out of him before pulling off the condom with some tissues at hand. He rolled over onto his back with a big smile on his face which I think mirrored mine for having such a good fuck.

'That was really wonderful Nicky,' he said, his eyes shining. 'I just hope that I can give the same pleasure to you.' I smiled back at him before leaning over him and taking the head of his cock into my mouth for a little sucking and chewing before rolling a condom down over it. With that on, he moved over on the bed for me to assume the position and when settled, he moved in between my open legs and stroked the cheeks of my bum first before holding my hip with his left hand. I didn't flinch as he had when I felt the head of his cock touch the entrance and made myself relax as he pushed himself forward and had the pleasure of that small bit of pain as he widened the entrance and felt the head move in to be quickly followed by the shaft as he filled me with his lovely throbbing organ.

With him fully inside, his other hand came to my hip and he began to fuck me, moving himself backwards and forwards. It was lovely to have a different person doing this for me to compare the technique between him and Rosie. There wasn't a lot of difference with the movement of a cock up your backside with it just going in and out, but it was other things, like making the cock twitch, the way your hips were held and the stroking of the waist with the hands. Just little things that made the difference.

Andria wasn't as good as Rosie in this, but I now loved a hard cock inside and fucking me irrespective of who it was behind doing the fucking. I loved the soothing massage that seemed to iron out the wrinkles and gave me peace of mind as well as pleasure. But this sexual act never lasted long with, I think, the duration usually being between two and three minutes of having an iron hard piece of flesh moving inside the back passage.

The tightening grip on my thighs and the fast movement was the prelude to his coming and then being held firm, his thighs tight up to the cheeks of my bum, he jerked away with grunts as he came inside me, finishing off with a big sigh as he leaned over my rear end.

'Nice and tight, Nicky,' he said. 'It was great.'

'That it was, Andria,' I replied and gave out the usual cry as I felt him pulling out for me to feel the air waft around my shrinking ring which always seemed so cold after the heat I had received.

I quickly turned round and used some tissues to pull off the condom as his cock was still hard and sticking out from his thighs as he sat back on his heels. With this lot dropped onto the floor, took the shiny head of his sperm covered cock into my mouth to suck and pull out the last remains of his cum as well as licking the head clean.

I flopped back onto the bed and opened my arms for him to move into for us to kiss after our fucking session, and this we did for nearly an hour until we were both hard, ready to fuck each other again before cuddling up to go to sleep. It was oral sex together when we woke up, loving that hard morning erection to suck and chew on and then get the flavour of his seed when we both finally came in our respective mouths.

***

They left after breakfast saying that next time, we should go to their place for dinner and sex though they admitted that their cooking was nowhere up to the standard of Rosie and myself. This we did a few weeks later when we had a night free from work and a few more times over the coming months, though we really gave them a shock one night.

That was because the pair of us went to the bar dressed up in our female gear. What a furore that caused when we entered and got many compliments from the regulars and were asked to have sex sessions with quite a few couples, accepting one or two at a later date. They too seemed to get a thrill at seeing us in our underwear and we had some good nights dressed up like this, but overall, it showed to us that we really preferred the union of us two.

***

We even began to go to our jobs dressed up as females and got quite a few comments about doing this, some good and some bad, getting called all kinds of names with the latter, I'll leave you to guess what they were. But we didn't care now as to who knew that we were gay.

We had been with the agency for three years before we had a change that helped us with our future aim of having our own restaurant. It was one of the few occasions that we were working together in quite a fashionable restaurant, dressed in our finery, preparing dinner and seeing that it was served up to our liking. The serving had almost come to an end when the maitre d' came into the kitchen.

'There's a Mr. Altman, an American oil magnate, who wishes to have some words with you,' he said to the two of us, and we both looked at each other, questions in our eyes. We took off the hair nets we wore whilst working with food and shook our heads to make our hair fall down which now settled nicely on our shoulders and checked each other so that we looked okay before going out to see this man.

The restaurant was still half full and we were led to which was the most prominent table of the place which had eight people sitting there. As we got closer, a middle aged man stood up as we approached and stopped just before him.

'I asked to see you to compliment you on one of the best meals I have ever had in London. It was superb,' he said, which brought smiles to our faces. 'Here's my card,' which he gave to me as I was standing closer to him. 'If you are free sometime tomorrow afternoon, I would like to have words with you. I'm staying at the Savoy.' I looked at Rosie who gave a slight nod of the head and I turned back to this magnate.

'Would three thirty be alright?' I asked.

'Excellent. I'll see you then,' he said, extending his hand which I shook and he also shook Rosie's before we went back to the kitchen.

'What do you think of that then?' Rosie asked.

'I think that he might, just might, be offering us a job,' I replied. 'We'll talk about this at home tonight. Let's get finished here first.'

And so we carried on till we finished and went home to our flat where we were soon undressed and in bed together.

'Well what do you think of this oilman?' Rosie asked after kissing my cheek, his hand running up and down my chest.

'I think he wants us to be of service to him,' I said.

'I like it when you service me,' he said with a giggle. I turned and kissed him.

'I like the meat you serve to me too,' I said, now rolling over on top of him, squashing my erect cock on his stomach alongside his erection as I gave him a deep open mouth kiss, letting our tongues play with each other.

It was a few minutes later that we began to service each other, something that we never tire of, using our erections to give pleasure to the both of us in the giving and receiving of it. The best fuck is the one that we have in the mornings with that iron bar of flesh at its hardest. We also liked the cleaning up process of sucking out the dregs of sperm as well as the licking of the exposed head with the foreskin pushed right back.

We only did the dinners at the restaurant so had the morning and afternoons free and it was after our lunch that we got dressed in our finest and took great care of our make-up before leaving to go to the Savoy. We presented ourselves at the desk just before the stipulated time and were told that we were expected and had a bell boy escort us up to the suite that this Mr. Altman occupied.

'That's what I like about you English. Punctual,' he greeted us with a big smile on his face and an outstretched hand. 'Thank you for coming, Miss Craig, or are you Miss Roznoir?' he asked still holding my hand.

'Actually it's Mr. Craig, me, and this is Mr. Roznoir,' I replied and he dropped my hand like a hot brick.

'You mean you're..........' He didn't really know what word to use as he looked at us dressed up as females, incredulity on his face.

'The word here in England is gay, Mr. Altman,' I said, giving him my best smile.

'Well this is certainly a surprise. I never dreamed.... thought that you were females. It's incredible! You certainly fooled me. But, well, I'm almost lost for words. Never mind, please sit down,' he said, indicating a sofa that was opposite to an armchair. 'Would you like a drink?'

'No thank you,' I said for the pair of us as we sat down. We had now a lot of practice in the way a woman moves, smoothing out the back of the dress before sitting down, keeping our legs together and not sprawling like a man with his legs apart.

'I'm still amazed,' he said, shaking his head slightly as he sat down opposite us. 'Do you....er,......'

'Yes. We sleep together and are partners in the full sense of the word,' I replied, now being able to say this without blushing in admitting that we fucked each other.

'Well it rather negates the question that I was going to ask. After such a wonderful meal last night, I was going to offer one of you a job of being my personal chef,' he said.

'Yes it does, for though we're not bookends, we are still a pair and will stay so. So if that was to be the question, the answer is no,' I said, starting to rise up from the sofa.

'Wait dammit! Sit down!' he said as an almost demand, looking somewhat flustered at my direct response. 'I....Godammit. Will you both work exclusively for me? It means a lot of travelling between the States, Europe and the Middle and Far East, though it's not for sightseeing. Business. Oil business. I have a couple of yachts that I use as an office outside of Europe and the East. My agent usually sets up the accommodation when I'm not staying at the ranch.

The pay will be comparative to your abilities though you won't be spending it as you'll be on expenses. Well? What do you say?'

'Thank you for the offer. Er, can Rosie and I talk this over first?' I replied.

'Certainly, but don't take too long for I'm flying out the day after tomorrow,' he said.

'Just a few minutes will do,' I answered.

'Okay,' he said getting up from his seat. 'I'll get myself a drink while you talk.' He went across the room to a small bar as I turned to Rosie.

'Well? What do you think of this?' I asked.

'It sounds like a dream come true,' he said in a low whisper, his eyes alight. 'Getting wages and not having to spend any of it. Saving it up for our real dream.'

'So we say yes then?' and he nodded and so I sat back and with Mr. Altman seeing this posture, came back over and sat down with his drink.

'You've decided then? What's the answer?' he asked, sitting forward.

'Yes, we'll take up the position of being your personal chefs,' I said back.

'Great!' He replied. 'You've got passports?'

'Er, no,' I said a little crestfallen at having to say this.

'Dammit!' He exclaimed and slumped back in his seat, taking a big swig from his glass before getting up and going over to a phone. He dialled a number and spoke a few words before coming back to us. 'I've asked my secretary to come in as I need a few details,' was all he was able to say before a door opened to the suite and a young man came in with a folder in his hand. Mr. Altman stood up and gestured for him to come closer.

'This is, er,.....'

'Rosie and my name is Nicky,' I supplied.

'And this is Thomas,' he said, introducing his secretary who we shook hands with. He then went on to tell Thomas that we were going to be his chefs as he called us, thankful that he didn't use the word cooks. He told him of the problem of passports and what was his itinerary in the near future. This he was told before turning back to us.

'A month. Can you get passports by then? he asked.

'I should think so,' I answered.

'Good. When you've got them, take them to the American Embassy for visas. Thomas, contact the embassy so that when they are presented that they are given visas immediately. Also book another two seats from now on when flying. Cable the "Marianne" and get the cook thrown off, okay?'

'Yes, sir,' Thomas replied, having written down his instructions in his notebook.

'Now give Thomas your phone number...'

'I'm sorry. We're not on the phone,' I said. 'But this number will be able to take any messages,' and I gave him my other home in Harrow.

'Fine. Thomas will pass on the date and flight number when we stop at Heathrow on our way to Kuwait.'

Kuwait! Rosie and I both looked at each other with smiles on our faces at this and I think that he was now looking forward to this as much as I was.

'Okay then. Welcome aboard,' Altman said, standing up and offering his hand. 'Till then, Nicky. Is that short for Nicholas?'

'Yes sir,' I replied.

'And Rosie?'

'It's really Georges sir. French,' said Rosie, 'But Rosie's a play on my surname the first part being Roz which in English is Rose.'

'Well seeing as you seem to dress the way you are, we'll keep it to Rosie and Nicky. Thanks for coming and agreeing to be my chefs.'

We shook hands with both him and Thomas before leaving the suite and as we were alone in the lift going back down to the lobby, we hugged each other in delight of the job we had landed and hoped that all will go well with it.

We didn't have time to go to our flat but went straight to the restaurant for our stint of cooking more delicious dinners for the diners, but, boy, didn't we really have a good fucking session when we did get home? Both of us were as happy as larks and couldn't wait to get our passports which we applied for the following day. We had to get these forms signed at the local police station showing them our birth certificates and giving our N.I. numbers to prove who we were in this application. The photos didn't take long and we soon gave these in for our passports.

We both went to our respective homes to tell our parents that we had finally taken on a job full time and mine were very happy for me in getting this position of working solely for an oil magnate. Rosie's parents were delighted too, though we both said that we couldn't stay overnight as we still had to work that evening in the restaurant.

Our next task was to inform the letting agents that we would be vacating the flat in four weeks time and also gave in our notice to the agency the same day. Now we just couldn't get the following days past us.

We even had Robina and Andria around for a dinner celebration one night and made it a foursome sex-wise that night. What joy that was to have a cock up the backside whilst sucking on another rampant cock and having your own sucked at the same time. Now that was pure heaven. Filled with semen in both holes and yet still giving out your own supply. Mind you, it took all night for each of us to have his turn being the recipient of this delicious form of sex.

*** *

It took three weeks for our passports to be received and we went straight to the American Embassy and they knew that we would be applying and it was Thomas whom we had to thank that we didn't have any problems there. The same day a telegram arrived from home asking me to give them a ring, which I did and dad passed over the message which was the date and time of the plane we were to catch at Heathrow airport.

During that last week, we took all that we wouldn't be needing to our homes and said our goodbyes, promising to write as often as we could. Even so, we still had two suitcases each, mostly with our female attire because we had to be dressed in male clothing because our passports stated that we were of that gender.

Our last night in the flat was just one long night of being serviced from behind, not forgetting the oral side of sex, fucking each other first in the kitchen, then the sitting room and finally in the bedroom. We even had it in the bathroom with one of us sitting on the pan as the other got astride and virtually impaled ourselves on the upright erection so that we could kiss and hold each other tight as we fucked in this way.

We were quite bleary eyed when we made our way to the airport the following morning. Not knowing, we queued before the booking in desk with other people only to find that we needn't have queued there at all for our tickets were waiting at the first class desk. Since it was first class, we didn't have to pay the excess weight with us having two suitcases each.

It was an hour spent in the waiting lounge, first class at that, and by holding Rosie's hand, I felt that he was trembling.

'It's my first time in a plane,' he stammered.

'Mine too, but let's enjoy it,' I said, while having collywobbles too though I didn't let him know that.

There were only two other people in the first class lounge and shortly after being given a fruit cocktail, free, we were the first to board the plane and shown into that section of the aircraft where we met up with Mr. Altman and Thomas and two other men that were travelling with them. We learned later that their names were Patrick Murphy and Richard Stirling, both ex-army and really bodyguards for Mr. Altman. The latter named man, though he used to be in the S.A.S., he wasn't related to the David Stirling who started that division of the army. I got to know him quite well later.

It was only a short stop for the aircraft and we were soon trundling down to the far end of the airfield where we had the thrill of actually being in a plane as it took off. Rosie, sitting next to me, held my hand tight as we felt the surge as the powerful engines roared and shot us down the runway to soar up in to the air and through the clouds into brilliant sunshine.

I had to prise my hand free from Rosie's strong grip when the plane settled down in its flight towards Kuwait and got a sickly smile from him as I did so.

'Wasn't that exciting?' I asked him, bubbling at the thrill.

'I was nearly sick,' he moaned, but brightened up once the aircraft was on an even keel and we were served drinks from a pretty stewardess. Though my whispering to Rosie that he looked much prettier than her when he was dressed up helped settle him down and I think, enjoyed the flight overall.

We were unable to speak to the others during the flight and, knowing our place in society, didn't approach Mr. Altman until he spoke to us after we had landed at Kuwait International Airport.

'Glad that you two made it,' he said, 'For I'm looking forward to having an excellent dinner tonight aboard the "Marianne".' This was the name of his yacht moored there.

This gave me trepidations as we didn't know the first thing about cooking aboard a ship let alone a yacht, and just hoped that they had the right kind of food and ingredients that we would need.

It was a stretch limousine that took us from the airport with our baggage and put us down at a stone jetty where a motor launch was waiting, which quickly took us out into the harbour to pull up by the gangway of a massive white yacht. It had three decks and found out later that it had twenty suites aboard and best of all, a magnificent kitchen. This was where I was corrected that the kitchen aboard any floating vessel is called the galley. But that was after one of the guards showed us the cabin I would be sharing with Rosie. This in itself was quite sumptuous. A double bed and its own toilet and shower and plenty of cupboard and drawer space.

When left alone inside, we hugged and kissed each other in this floating hotel of sorts and quickly undressed, out of the now hated male clothing and had a quick session sucking each other's erection, having our first sex on board before getting dressed up in our female attire.

Sexually satisfied and dressed as we now liked being dressed, we made our way to the galley to find that we had a helper there which was a godsend. He saw to the basic rudiments of a kitchen, such as peeling potatoes and preparing vegetables as well as doing all the washing up afterwards. He was an Arabian by the name of Daoud, though he wasn't quite sure in what country he was born in, he held a Kuwaiti passport.

We found that the yacht was well stocked, which pleased us and it wasn't long before Thomas appeared to tell us that there would be sixteen for dinner in the dining room and that there was a total of fourteen crew members to be fed as well. This involved setting up two menus every day, one for the guests and one for the crew, for we didn't think it would go down very well if the crew were to eat the same sumptuous meals that we would be expected to serve up. Though we did make two exceptions to this, that being Daoud and Phillip, who was the dining room steward, who also doubled up as the barman when not serving the meals. These two we had to keep happy to help us make a success of this undertaking, and it worked, for we got along fine.

I was rather dubious about what we should serve up with this being our first meal aboard this yacht and having to make a good impression, I decided, after looking at what was stored aboard, chose Lobster Thermidor as the main course.

Now this is a meal that takes time to prepare but I knew we would have just enough and so that is what we went for, and without blowing my own trumpet, it was a great success. Mr. Altman couldn't praise us enough afterwards and even had us go into the saloon to be applauded by all those that had dined at the table.

We were then the best thing since sliced bread. Even Phillip and Daoud said that they had never eaten such a fine meal, mind you, we ate the same as they did. Well, what would you expect?

Where we had the main dining room on one side of the kitchen, on the other side we had the crew's mess room, and we then found out that they had two sittings because they always had to have at least one man up on the bridge, well two really. The man in charge and the helmsman, and with the engine room, another man had to stay on duty while the chief engineer had his meal. It was then that I noticed that one of the body guards had his meal separate from his colleague as one was always on hand even in the dining room, though not actually eating with the guests, but more or less somewhere there in the background. This I found out when I finally bedded Richard Stirling. I didn't know at our first meeting that he was a man to go for male sex, but I was proven wrong, for he hit upon me only after having been on board a week.

'Nicky,' he began one evening after dinner had been seen to. 'Will you come and have a drink with me?' It was only then that I knew that he wanted sex with me. I was right about his age, guessing that he was about forty odd years old and as he was good looking, also looked like a man who knew how to handle himself. I also hoped that he could handle me in the right way when I accepted his offer.

I think that Rosie was a bit miffed that I was asked for a drink and he had come to the same conclusion that I had already formulated. So I went along to his cabin which he shared with Patrick and found that we would be alone having this drink for Patrick was now on duty.

'Rum, whisky, gin or vodka?' he asked when I sat down on his bunk after entering the cabin.

'Gin and tonic please,' I said, settling down and waited for his approach, which wasn't long in coming. He passed me my drink and sat down next to me with his, and I waited as I sipped my drink for him to make the first move. Though to tell you the truth, I did want him to.

'You surprised both Patrick and myself when we first saw you on the plane coming out to Kuwait being dressed in male clothing and then seeing you aboard wearing a dress. Are you bi-sexual or homosexual?' I was wearing a dress with the usual underwear at the time.

'Both,' I lied, me not yet having had the experience of getting my end away with a woman.

'So am I,' he said. 'Though I am more of a man to be the one to give rather than receive if you know what I mean.'

'Well as you've brought the question up so fast, the only thing I can say is that I don't mind the not fucking side of it, but if you are not prepared to suck then I'll finish this drink and go.' I was really laying down the rule here. If he wanted to fuck me, he had to respond by at least sucking on me. Well, it's only fair don't you think?

'Well, Nicky. I've never sucked on another man......'

'No suck. No fuck. It's as simple as that. I don't mind you fucking me but it's not going to be one sided if you know what I mean. Rosie and I both fuck and suck each other and she's quite miffed that I've left her alone tonight to come into your cabin.'

'Well she...he can always get together with Darren, the second engineer. He's, er, somewhat of the same persuasion that you two are,' he said rather lamely. This gave me food for thought that if Rosie was to be able to have this Darren, he couldn't really object to me having Richard who obviously wanted to fuck me. Looking at Richard sitting next to me, he looked like a strong man and not that bad looking either, but I was going to stick to my guns, no suck, no fuck.

'How long will we be on this yacht?' I asked.

'I think for another five days, why?'

'Well you seem to travel all the time with the boss, but the second engineer won't,' I countered with.

'I've been with the boss as you call him for the past year and know of many men at places that we've stopped at who would just love to have Rosie in bed with them.'

'Okay. You seemed to have sorted out the problem of Rosie, but what about us? Okay, I can see your hesitation, but it is still a suck or no fuck. You can spit it out if you want, but then you'll never know the true meaning of love even without being fucked.' The ball was now back in his court. It took a few moments before he acquiesced to me demands.

'Okay, I agree,' he said. 'Let me fuck you and then I'll give you a suck, okay?'

'No. You suck on me first and then I'll let you fuck me,' I countered with. 'We're not playing chicken here.'

'Okay,' he said with a wry grin on his face, and I passed him my glass and stood up and slipped the straps of my dress off my shoulders and let it slither down my body to show me in my female underwear but with a full erection jutting out in front of me. I stepped out of the puddle of my dress and picked it up and laid it over a chair and sat down next to him and waited for him to make the next move.

He surprised me by getting up from the bed and instead of going down on me there and then, took all his clothes off and showed me exactly what I thought had been hidden inside his trousers. A nice big, large and lengthy organ and I couldn't stop myself from reaching out and taking hold of it and pulling him forward for me to take that glorious looking cock head into my mouth. I only gave him a brief suck and chew before letting go of that wonderful tool he had and pointed down to my erection that was sticking upright from between my female clad thighs.

It seemed that he gave out a sigh as he went down onto his knees and I saw that he licked his lips first before opening his mouth and took the head of my cock inside. No way was he a cocksucker, but I suppose it was his first time and I think it was this that made me come sooner than I would have liked, but come I did. He gave a snort as the first surge hit his upper palate and took the rest without any noise until I'd finished coming and we was also quick to pull his head back and spit out that lovely semen of mine that I know Rosie would have run it round his mouth before swallowing. But he was a tyro in this form of sex, but at least he had sucked on me and therefore earned his right to now fuck me.

'That was lovely, Richard,' I lied, 'Though when Rosie and I do it to each other, we swallow what comes out, but I'll forgive you since this is your first time. Now you can fuck me,' I said, as I then got up onto the bed proper and bent forward on my knees and waited to have that lovely organ that I had seen, given to me in the right place.

He was quickly up behind me and rammed himself into me without any finesse and what was more, he wasn't even wearing a condom, but, what the fuck, I didn't care for I just loved being fucked bareback, to be able to feel the real man behind doing what I loved being done to me, and then to be able to feel the spurting semen spraying my insides.

He was quite vigorous in moving himself in and out of my back passage as he fucked away and I was filled, not only with his cock, but joy at having another man shaft me in this fashion. I even crooned out for him to move harder, loving the smacking of his thighs up to the cheeks of my bum. It was even better as he started to come, gripping my hips even tighter as he pulled me back onto his forward thrusting until he held me firm as only his hips jerked away as he sent his sperm up into my backside.

I was in heaven again at having a strong male penis up inside me, creaming my insides with his coming, loving the thrill it gave me, and sighed when he came to a halt, his cock still throbbing away where I liked it most. But gave out that cry as the toy that had just pleased me was being pulled out for me to feel the cool air waft round my shrinking arsehole.

'Thank you, Nicky, I needed that,' he panted as he sat back on his heels.

'I needed it too,' I said, turning round, 'And if you'd worn a condom I'd be sucking on you now. Go and wash yourself and do it properly.'

He gave a sigh and me a smile before getting off the bed and going off into his bathroom. His body was strong with solid thighs, a nice shaped bum and big shoulders that had muscled arms attached. I found out later that the yacht boasted a small gym and it was there that he worked out and kept his muscles toned. He looked even better from the front when he returned from the bathroom. His muscled chest, lightly covered in hair and a fairly trim waist and a nice flaccid dick hanging between his thighs which swayed about as he got back onto the bed.

He fell on top of me and kissed me which was a surprise for I didn't expect this from him, but it was only lip kissing, not an open mouth one. It took me a few minutes to get him to roll off onto his back so that I could move down the bed and take the whole length of his deflated dick into mouth to suck and chew on. He gave out a groan as I did so and I think he enjoyed what I was doing for he stroked my hair while I was down on him.

I didn't stay long in his cabin for I knew that Rosie was upset at me going off with Richard and so when I got to our cabin, I took Rosie around the world sex-wise, which pleased him.

***

We had just finished serving up lunch when Thomas came into the galley.

'The boss wants to see you,' he said to us both and we duly followed him into the now empty dining room except for Mr. Altman sitting there.

'Well my two sea girls, you did me proud with the meals while here which I think helped our talks. We're off tomorrow after breakfast, so be packed and ready. Thomas will give you the details.'

With that being said, he got up and left the dining room where Thomas then told us that a private jet had been placed at the boss's service and we would be flying off to Houston, Texas. This thrilled us and next morning, leaving the cleaning up after breakfast to Phillip and Daoud, we left with the others to be escorted to this private jet that was soon in the air on the way to the States.

There was only the six of us and we had plenty of space in this ten-seater plane, being served by a lovely looking stewardess. I noticed later during the flight that both she and Mr. Altman disappeared into what looked like a small cabin at the rear of the plane and from the look on his face later, guessed that he'd fucked her back there.

I whispered to Rosie who was sitting next to me of what I think went on at the back and wished that we could do the same. He grinned and wished we could too, but we didn't, but some time later we had the chance in another plane and we went and joined the mile high club by fucking each other miles up in the sky, but that was later.

Eight hours out from Kuwait, we landed in America, another first for us and cars were waiting to whisk us off to a lovely big apartment where we would be staying. It was back to work for us as it had its own kitchen where we cooked up and served dinner to the rest.

Mr. Altman was often out with the other three on business leaving Rosie and myself alone, but always returned for dinner which we had ready for them. But when the cat's away, we mice played. Read that as having each other twice during that free time we had.

During that week we stayed there, Richard fucked me twice and Rosie once, for he said that he preferred me to Rosie but I had insisted that he saw to him as well as me. That was the pattern we set and carried on like this for a whole year as we travelled all over the world in the service of Mr. Altman, saving all our bloody good wages which was piling up nicely for our future restaurant.

We went to many out of the way places where there was oil like Borneo, Venezuela, Indonesia and many more as well as staying quite often in the States and England. It was during this year that we turned Thomas into being bi-sexual as was Richard, by getting him to fuck Rosie while I was being fucked by Richard, which meant that neither of us two went without sex and not be alone at night in bed. Richard quite often then, slept in bed with me and Rosie went and slept with Thomas, but it was Rosie and myself together most nights.

As much as I loved Rosie, I liked the bodily hardness of Richard, a real man in all senses of the word. Strong in both character and mind and had a nice big cock when it was fully erect. Though I didn't get to fuck him, he at least sucked on me and eventually got around to swallowing my cum instead of spitting it out.

Then came an event which changed things somewhat. We got involved in a hijack.

***

We were once again in Kuwait on board the yacht "Marianne", and with the boss's business finished there, had the yacht set course for Durban where he had more business to attend to. He used the yacht as he wanted to have a long rest for a change and so that was to be our destination. It would take us just under fourteen days covering just over five thousand nautical miles.

Mr. Altman had since acquired a girlfriend, i.e., bed mate, and so we had twenty-one people aboard, so we only had three to serve in the main dining room and eighteen in the mess room for the crew, that last total was including us galley staff and the two bodyguards. The mess room had two sittings because the bridge, engine room and a bodyguard still had to be on attendance whilst at sea.

The bridge and engine had two shifts, them changing every eight hours whilst the bodyguards took turns between day and night at being on hand. We were six days out of Kuwait and somewhere off the Somalia coast. It was after dinner and Rosie had gone off to Thomas's cabin while I had Richard in with me for he was on the day shift this week.

He liked seeing me pull off my dress for him to see me in my lingerie and I got onto the bed and lay back with my erection lying up on my stomach as I watched him undress. His naked body shone in the dim bed light, nice and bronzed from his sunbathing, his cock sticking out nice and hard and it waved about as he got onto the bed with me.

We varied the sequence of when he sucked on me, preferring it after he had fucked me, and so I moved down and took the head of his cock into my mouth, pushing the foreskin down with my lips. Now I could really tease the G-spot and make him tremble with delight in the sensations it gave him. I also gently nibbled the bare flesh as I sucked before releasing him and slowly nibbled my way down the length of his shaft and made him quiver again when I took his balls into my mouth to agitate the growing sperm inside them.

I didn't do this for long as I wanted this hard piece of flesh up inside me and so released him and got out a condom and rolled it right down over his cock and moved around and up onto my knees. He had said that he just loved fucking me as I liked him doing it too. The entry was lovely, feeling every inch of him as he slowly slid inside till his sturdy thighs, came up to my bum cheeks and could not get any further inside me. My muscle kept flexing away at his shaft, making his cock twitch inside before he began to move and slowly massage my canal from the inside.

I always seemed to drool when I had such a length of this hard flesh moving inside me, such was the pleasure I got from being reamed.

Though like always, this pleasure doesn't last long and he was soon holding my hips tight in his hands as he began to ram himself hard into me as he also pulled my body back onto his. Then came his shuddering as only his hips jerked away as he came inside me, and I could hear his panting and grunts as he shot his load. He then leaned over my back and even in the coolness of the cabin with its air conditioning, he was still sweating as I felt drops land on my lower back.

'As lovely as ever,' he panted, giving my waist a squeeze and began to pull out to my cries of dismay as this happened, the most hated part of the coupling to my mind. I quickly grabbed some tissues and pulled off the used condom and went down on him to suck out what was left and licked the head clean before falling back for him to then see to me.

With it being quite cool in the cabin, I pulled the covers right up because I was feeling somewhat chilled as he came under the covers and slid down the bed until his head was lying on my stomach as he took me into his mouth to suck and chew on my throbbing cock. His hand worked on me as he sucked and it didn't take long for me to send my seed into his mouth which he swallowed and then began licking me clean.

He was just about finished when the door to the cabin was suddenly crashed open and the main light turned on. I shot up onto my elbows and I felt Richard freeze beneath the covers.

In the doorway stood a swarthy unkempt man with a sub machine pistol pointing at me.

'Get up,' he snarled at me, waving the gun to indicate me to get out of bed. His English was bad but I understood his demand. 'Get up and get dressed,' he said. I felt Richard give my thigh a pinch and as he hadn't moved, I guessed he wanted to stay hidden beneath the bed covers. It was a bit difficult to get out of bed yet leave him covered, but I managed it. The man gave out a laugh when he saw that I was wearing my female underwear and was still chuckling when I picked up my dress off the chair and put it on. His eyes were on me all the time and so never noticed the hump still under the covers.

He prodded me out of the cabin with his gun and I went as directed with the poking gun until we were up in the lounge. There I found half of our crew already there being covered by another two gunmen as more of the crew were pushed in to join us until we were all twenty of us were assembled. The odd one not being there was Richard. This was noticed by the boss and I managed to sidle up to him and whispered that they missed Richard and to warn the others that he was at the moment, undiscovered. He knew straight away that he would be our only hope and therefore managed to speak to the others in not mentioning him at all.

We were now being covered by five gunmen, all swarthy looking Arabs as we sat and didn't stop us from talking quietly to each other. It was obviously a hijacking and we were now hostages for whatever ransom they were going to demand. Being off the Somalian coast, it was assumed that they were from this country. I heard the yacht's captain tell Mr. Altman that it seemed that there were at least eight of them that had come alongside in two black motorised dinghies and boarded from two sides, catching those on the bridge unawares.

We all looked rather miserable for the rest of the night, sitting there in the lounge until daylight, being questioned as to who was in charge of the boat and finding out that it was Mr. Altman who was told that we and the yacht would be putting in toward the coast where we would be held until ransomed.

When it was fully daylight, the apparent leader of these men wanted to know who was the cook on board and Rosie and I slowly raised our hands and we were then ordered to cook a meal for them and those in the lounge. It was here that we found out that there was indeed eight men holding us hostage. There was some laughter from these men when the one that had got me out of my cabin spoke to them, though they spoke in Arabic, I understood that he was telling them that I was actually a man dressed up as a woman. One even grabbed Rosie and put his hand up to his crotch and laughed out loud at feeling male genitalia there too. This made them all laugh again as we were pushed at gunpoint, out of the lounge and into the galley to start cooking everybody breakfast.

We asked if we could have another to help us and it was agreed and I pointed at Daoud, but as they could see that he too was Arabian and spoke the language, wouldn't let him come with us and so we had Phillip.

In whispers, we found out that he had been told that Richard was at large and so he wasn't mentioned again as we cooked breakfast for all aboard. They all ate in the lounge with their plates on their laps. The hijackers took turns to eat, the one looking after us made sure that we didn't add anything strange to the meals that they would eat.

After the meal and with the things washed up, we were ushered back out into the lounge and there we stayed until lunchtime. It was the same process as at breakfast and the next time we were allowed in the galley was to prepare for dinner. I went in early to get food and things from the storeroom which was next to the galley. I had one man guard me and he followed me into where the stores were kept.

When inside, he gave me a push towards the table that was in there and then forced me to lay forward over it. I guessed why he did this and wasn't surprised when I felt the hem of my dress being lifted up and pushed up onto my back, leaving my bum bare. I felt him moving behind me and guessed that he had slung his gun over his shoulders as I now felt one hand on my hip and I heard him spit and guessed that his was lubricating his cock and his other hand then came onto my other hip and felt the head of his cock nestle to my rear entrance. There was no finesse for he just shoved his erect cock straight up into me and began his movement in fucking me. There was nothing I could do to stop him, not that I really wanted to, for he was quite big in that department and it gave me a weird kind of thrill to be fucked by this Arab terrorist.

It wasn't a bad fuck from this man and he was soon really ramming himself up against my backside as he began to grunt at each shot of his seed being sent up into me and finally came to a stop leaning over me and then came a loud thump and he fell onto my back and slowly slid down from me, his cock sliding out too.

I turned my head as he was falling away from me to see a grinning Richard looking at me and my bare bum.

'I would rather had done that instead of him,' he said as he bent down and turned the terrorist over and gave him another big thump at the throat. I had straightened up now, my dress covering me once again. I had watched him in horror as he had struck the man at the throat.

'You could kill him doing that,' I said.

'That was the intention,' he said. 'So that's one less. Do you know how many there are?'

'Eight,' I said. 'Including him,' pointing to the man on the deck.

'Seven left then,' he said as he began pulling the gun free and slinging it over his shoulder. 'Perfect,' he said when he found two grenades in the man's jacket pockets. 'Stun grenades. Here, take them,' he said, handing them to me.

'What will I do with them,' I said when he gave them to me. 'Where will I put them? I've got no pockets in this dress.'

'You're wearing a bra. Stuff them in the cups,' he said. 'Now listen carefully. I know that two are on the bridge at the moment and one down in the engine room. That leaves four of them to guard you all. Tonight, there will be only one on the bridge and one in the engine room. Two I think would be guarding you while the others sleep. Now I am going to take care of those not in the lounge and I want you to take care of the two that will be guarding you.'

'Me! How?' I demanded.

'Stay awake and as close to five in the morning as you can, I want you to pull the pins out of these grenades and roll them towards the terrorists. You'll have five seconds before they explode. Don't worry, they will only stun you. It won't be so bad if when you've thrown them, close your eyes and keep your mouth open. That way you won't suffer.' Liar, I found out later.

'I'll be outside when they go off and I will then come in and take care of them.'

'How will you see to those not in with us?' I stupidly asked.

'I didn't spend all those years with the commandos not to know how to deal with them. Now killing this man here has given me a hard on which I'd like you to see to.' He had a big smile on his face as he pulled this erection out of his trousers and I couldn't get down on my knees quick enough at seeing this rampant cock wanting service. It was only later that I reflected at how insensitive I had been in kneeling down next to a dead man while I sucked on another man's cock, but then the man had just fucked me without asking which was really rape, so this I think absolved me for not caring about him.

Mind you, it was lovely sucking on Richard's throbbing cock and the emission I got went smoothly down my throat when he came inside my mouth. After licking him clean, I got up as he put himself away.

'How do I explain that this guard is missing?' I asked of Richard.

'Just say that he went out through the mess room and don't know where he went. I'll get rid of his body where they won't find him,' and guessed that he was going to dump him over the side.

I gave Richard a kiss and he didn't seem to mind kissing the lips that had only just come up from being around the head of his cock. I went back out into the galley with the things that I had gone into the store for. With these placed ready, I went back into the lounge to collect Rosie and Phillip to help getting dinner ready.

'Where's Ahmed?' I was asked by their leader.

'Who?' I asked, knowing exactly whom he was talking of.

'The man guarding you. Where is he?'

'I don't know. He went off through the mess room, but where to, I've no idea,' I said. He then gave out a torrent of Arabic which I didn't understand and shrugged my shoulders as I called out for the other two to give me help in the galley. Another man was sent to guard and watch over our cooking. It was very uncomfortable for me having these two grenades stuffed into the bra cups as they kept rubbing against my chest with every move I made. But I suffered them knowing that they would help us later to be free of these villains.

There was some muttering amongst these guards when they ate at different times and guessed that it was about the disappearing Ahmed. With dinner finally over and the things cleaned up, we all settled down to sleep in the lounge and as Richard had predicted, we had two different guards watching over us, guessing that they had slept sometime during the day to be able to stay awake for the night.

I had opted to sleep on the carpeted deck quite near to where the guards were sitting with their guns across their laps. I had pulled Rosie with me and we lay down side by side and it was when all were settled down that I whispered to Rosie what had occurred earlier, well nearly all, leaving out the fucking and sucking part. His eyes were wide open upon hearing that Richard killed the guard and they widened even more when I slipped the two grenades out of my bra and lay on them till five o'clock in the morning.

I didn't get to sleep at all I was that wound up and from where I was lying, I could see the clock on the wall of the lounge and watched the hands slowly make their way round the face until it was a couple of minutes to the hour. I gently prodded Rosie awake and she knew what was about to happen and what I wanted her to do. I got the grenades out from the uncomfortable place I had put them and held down both the clips for Rosie to pull out the locking pins.

I let go of the clips, hearing them click and counted to three and quickly tossed them towards the two guards. One had been dozing and the other suddenly sat up as they bounced towards them. I then laid my head down on the carpet with my eyes closed and mouth open as they exploded.

Christ! The blast nearly split my ear drums but didn't knock me out and saw Richard burst into the lounge and with a short burst of gunfire, killed both of the guards. What pandemonium we had there then with half of our people knocked out and the other crying out at the pain to their ears.

I was up quickly and went over to Richard who was just checking to see that the two men were indeed dead and straightened up satisfied that they were.

'The others?' I asked in rather a loud voice for my ears were still ringing and couldn't control my voice.

'Dead. All of them. We've now got control again of the yacht.'

He quickly went over then to see to Mr. Altman who had just groggily risen up from the couch where he had been sleeping and Richard told him that we were now all free and had his hand shaken in thanks.

With everybody now coming around, the captain quickly had the engineers sent below and he and two others of the crew went off to the bridge. It was only a couple of minutes later that we felt the yacht heel over onto a new course and could feel that they had also increased the speed to get us out of the Somalian sea limits.

By the time that everybody had been able to return to their cabins for showers and shaves etc. Rosie and I began to see to getting an early breakfast ready and it wasn't until after the meal that I was called out to speak with Richard and Mr. Altman.

It was Richard who spoke first, telling the boss how I had helped him by first, concealing him in my cabin, to which I guess that the boss knew that he'd only been in there for sex with me, but didn't comment on this as Richard continued. By staying concealed, he was able to move about in various hiding places until he caught the first guard in the store room, omitting that I was being fucked by him at the time, and killing him and throwing his body over the side.

He told of giving me the grenades and the instructions as to how and when to use them. During the night he first took out the man at the helm and then the man in the engine room. Next was to find the sleeping ones in various cabins knowing the total of men from me, knew that the last two were in the lounge. That it was my using the grenades that helped him take these two out without any loss of life from our side.

'Well I must really congratulate the pair of you for what you have done. You Richard for acting as you did and you Nicky for your assistance. I will see that you both are suitably rewarded when we get Stateside for you have undoubtedly saved me several million dollars if not more. Congratulations once again,' he said as he shook our hands. Richard went off to go to sleep while I had to slug away in the gallery and by dinner time, I could hardly keep my eyes open and Rosie made me go down to our cabin for he would see to the rest of dinner for which I was thankful and as soon as my head hit the pillow, I was asleep.

Rosie, bless him, didn't wake me when he came off duty and got into bed with me without disturbing me but woke me up in the best fashion in the morning by having my morning erection in his mouth, sucking away. I gave out a pleasurable groan as I stretched while he sucked and came with some force into his mouth which I think he enjoyed. Well I enjoyed my turn in going down on him and taking all of his emission to roll around my mouth before swallowing.

It was a happy yacht full of people this next day that we had gotten away so lightly from these hijackers and come the end of dinner, I asked Rosie if he would go to Thomas's cabin as I really had to thank Richard in the only way I knew. He understood and went off and I didn't have any problem in getting Richard to come into mine that night.

'I want to really thank you for saving us,' I said as I helped him off with his clothes and quickly went down and gave his erection a quick few sucks before slipping my dress off and getting onto the bed on my knees.

'And I want to thank you for the help you gave me from the beginning,' he said as he pushed himself up into my backside.

'Thank heaven, for nice big boys,' I crooned, singing that famous song but putting different words as he moved himself in and out of me, 'they rise up in the most delightful way.' Then he began to sing in not a bad voice, the same song with different words too.

'Thank heaven, for girls like you, you pleasure me in everything you do,' and we both started to laugh at this and it brought him to a stop and I had to move myself back onto him to remind him where he was and what he should be doing to this sea girl. So back to the job in hand, as the saying goes, but the job wasn't in hand but up inside me, and I gurgled away in delight as I felt him start to come inside me. What delight to feel it throbbing away and the exquisite jerks the head of his cock gave as it ejected his seed albeit into the condom, though I really did like being fucked bareback to actually feel it splash my channel.

After the hated pulling out and feeling my ring puckering up as I pulled off the soiled condom and taking as much of his erect piece of meat into my mouth to finish off the job. Then I had the pleasure of him sucking on me till I came and could see that he did in fact like doing this to me now whereas he hadn't at first.

So for the rest of the following week I was being fucked by Richard and fucked by Rosie who I was able to fuck in return on our trip down to Durban. With our safe arrival there, we left the yacht having heard the boss tell the captain to give Somalia a wide berth on his return trip to Kuwait where the yacht was based.

Rosie and I were given some time off, three days really for we stayed over two days in a hotel and so we didn't do any cooking while the boss saw to his business in the dealing of oil. Rosie and I both sent off postcards to home as we did from every new city that we visited and when the boss finally finished his business, we flew off to the States to finish up on the huge ranch that he owned.

We spent a week there assisting the cook that lived on the ranch, learning the way that the Texans liked their steaks and fritters. We only tried once at the riding of a horse but gave it up not really knowing how to handle one. It was on our third day there that the boss asked me into his study.

'Well my favourite sea girl,' he began, offering me the chair before his desk while he went and sat down behind it. 'The pleasure of being behind this desk again is due to you and Richard. I've given him a suitable reward for taking back the yacht though he said that without your help, he wouldn't have been able to succeed. What could I give you that you desire most of all?'

With that question being asked, I took the bull by the horns.

'A restaurant in London that I could give it the name of Marianne's,' I said, my heart in my mouth. I'd deliberately picked the name of the yacht, as I had found out earlier that it was also the name of his late mother after whom the yacht had been named.

'Not necessarily give, but be a partner where you and your guests would be treated to the finest of meals but at no charge whenever you are in London.' The palms of my hand were sweating now as he leaned back in his chair and studied me for a few minutes while he thought this over in his mind.

'So you want to leave me? Desert me?' he said.

'No! Not really, but it is the dream of Rosie and I to have our own place and in taking on the position of being your chefs was to earn enough money to buy such a place. It's....it's just that you have now just given me a chance, a chance to realise that dream earlier than we thought.' I shut up then, for I didn't think I could put it any better and the least said etc.

'Hmm,' he muttered. 'Give me a day or two to mull this over. Partner you say?'

'Yes, sir,' my heart beating wildly that he hadn't turned me down straight away.

'I'll think about it,' he said and I knew it was time for me to leave his study, so I stood up and thanked him and left. I kept it to myself for the time being as I would rather tell Rosie later in bed.

I got Rosie to fuck me first, soothing my inner passage as he normally did when inside me, loving his movements that gave me pleasure and thrill as I felt him come inside me as he rode me bareback. I groaned as usual at his withdrawal, hating the loss of that lovely organ that I worshipped and fell forward on the bed as he left it to go and wash himself.

With him getting back into the bed, I moved so that he could assume the normal position we used for this form of sex and I got behind him and between his legs. I bent down and gave each cheek of his bum a kiss before straightening up and pushing my erection into that lovely orifice to give him the same pleasure that he had given me.

I just loved riding him bareback, feeling the heat of his body surrounding my cock and having his muscle keep squeezing me as I moved slowly backwards and forwards in his heavenly cavern. I even teased him by pulling right out before pushing myself back inside him to his gurgles of dismay and joy at the withdrawal and re-entry. But nature takes over and I was soon holding him tight to my thighs as I pumped out my semen into him, getting little cries of delight at every spurt that I'm sure he felt.

I came to a halt, leaning heavily against his rear as I panted, gathering my breath back before pulling out knowing that he hated this part as much as I did. But out I came and went off to the bathroom to wash myself very carefully.

It was then onto the bed and into his waiting arms I went for a kiss and cuddle and as we settled down, I told him of what I had said to the boss.

He gave out a cry of delight and an instant erection at the possible thought of our own restaurant in the very near future. Me, feeling his cock rise up so quickly, caused mine to rise up too, even though I'd just fucked him a few minutes earlier, I was up as hard as he was and so he turned round on the bed and got us into the sixty-nine position so that we could both suck on each other at the same time.

For nearly an hour we sucked and chewed, well nibbled really, on each other, not forgetting to take the lovely pair of balls into our mouths to gently move them about in their sac. That was a lovely hour in doing this and when nearing our peaks, to take the bare head in to suck and wait for the surge of seed that we soon gave to each other to savour before swallowing.

***

Rosie fairly bubbled for the rest of the short time we were at the ranch, for the day before we left, the boss called me into his study again to give me the news that he agreed to buy a restaurant or place that could be turned into one. The task for this he had given to Thomas to use several agents to find such a place in a most fashionable area. But, he had said, this would take time and if the place found had to be converted, it could take as long as a year. I was over the moon with this news as was Rosie when I told him. What was one more year to us? Nothing, considering we were still only in our mid-twenties and had expected to work for quite a few years before we had enough money to buy a place of our own. I think it was having told the boss that the name for the restaurant would be Marianne's that swayed him though by doing so knew that he would lose us as his chefs, well he would have done eventually.

***

We had left the ranch and was once again travelling around the world visiting new places as well as some that we had been to before, though the thrill of this was on the wane. The only thing that kept our spirits buoyed up was the sex we had together, was getting even better as time passed. We still had our flings too, me with Richard and him with Thomas.

We'd been away from the ranch a month before Thomas, on the side, told us that an agent had found what could be the perfect place for us and contrived the boss's itinerary for us to stop over in London. It was in a small side street in Belgravia that was admirable both in size and location and Thomas had the power to set things in motion in the purchase, leasehold, and of getting a reputable firm to turn the place into our work place and dream home for it would also include the apartments above. It was a feverish week for us there in drawing up rough plans of how we wanted the interior set up but left the interior designs to others to work their magic. Ten months was the estimated time and this time period seemed to lag for us as we carried on being the chefs for Mr. Altman.

But the time eventually arrived when we were told that the place was ready and the boss made it a point for us to return to London to see the finished premises. It was a dream of a place and a contract was drawn up between us that he, the boss, would receive two thirds of the profits for the first year. Half for the second and a third for the third year, after which, it was ours with the provision that he got free meals at every visit. This we agreed to and we signed on the dotted line and a week later, left the employment roster of Mr. Altman.

In that last week, I spent every night in bed with Richard to say our goodbyes as Rosie did with Thomas. As much as I loved Rosie, I still had a certain amount left over for Richard, that hulk of a man that had muscles like I'd never seen on another man, and with a cock that had given me so much pleasure.

Mr. Altman and the others didn't stay for the opening as it would be at least two weeks for us to get in some decent staff and all the necessary foodstuff. It was also a painful time for both Rosie and myself to tell our parents that we were both gay and would be living together.

Mum cried when I told them after dinner the night I stayed over at home. Dad accepted it philosophically adding that he still considered me to be his son and loved me in spite of what I had said. Mum finally came around to accept the fact that I was in love with another man though the subject of our having sex was not mentioned.

The night we opened was a private affair having my parents and some of their friends and it was the first time that they met the parents of Rosie. They seemed to get on okay though the fact that both sets of parents now knew that Rosie and I were lovers, it wasn't mentioned. Rosie's parents had also brought along a few friends, so we had twelve guests to be served up the best we could produce for this opening night.

The plaudits were high and pleased us very much but it was a relief when they all left and after the staff we employed had cleaned up, we closed down and went up to our new apartments. Here, we fell into each other's arms to kiss and complement each other on a successful evening.

It was a lovely apartment we had above the restaurant with all mod cons and a lovely big bed into which we went and it was sheer heaven at having got past our opening night and could now really relax and enjoy ourselves in the loving we had to give to each other. The thrill of being dressed up as females and of seeing each other in this attire when the dresses came off. To stroke and fondle the erections we had and then to be able to use it in the right place, up inside each other.

The pleasure of being inside Rosie, slowly stroking the inner canal as I moved both my body on him and run my hands up and down his waist, hearing him croon out his pleasure as I shafted him. Then had the extra joy at having him inside me, giving me the same pleasure as he fucked me until his seed surged up and out for me to feel it.

This was our heaven and we made the most of it and the finishing touch was that I had bought a sprig of mistletoe which was now hung above our bed and what we couldn't stop giggling over was that one such as this was what had brought us together in our happiness.

The End

Here is a sample from another story you may enjoy:

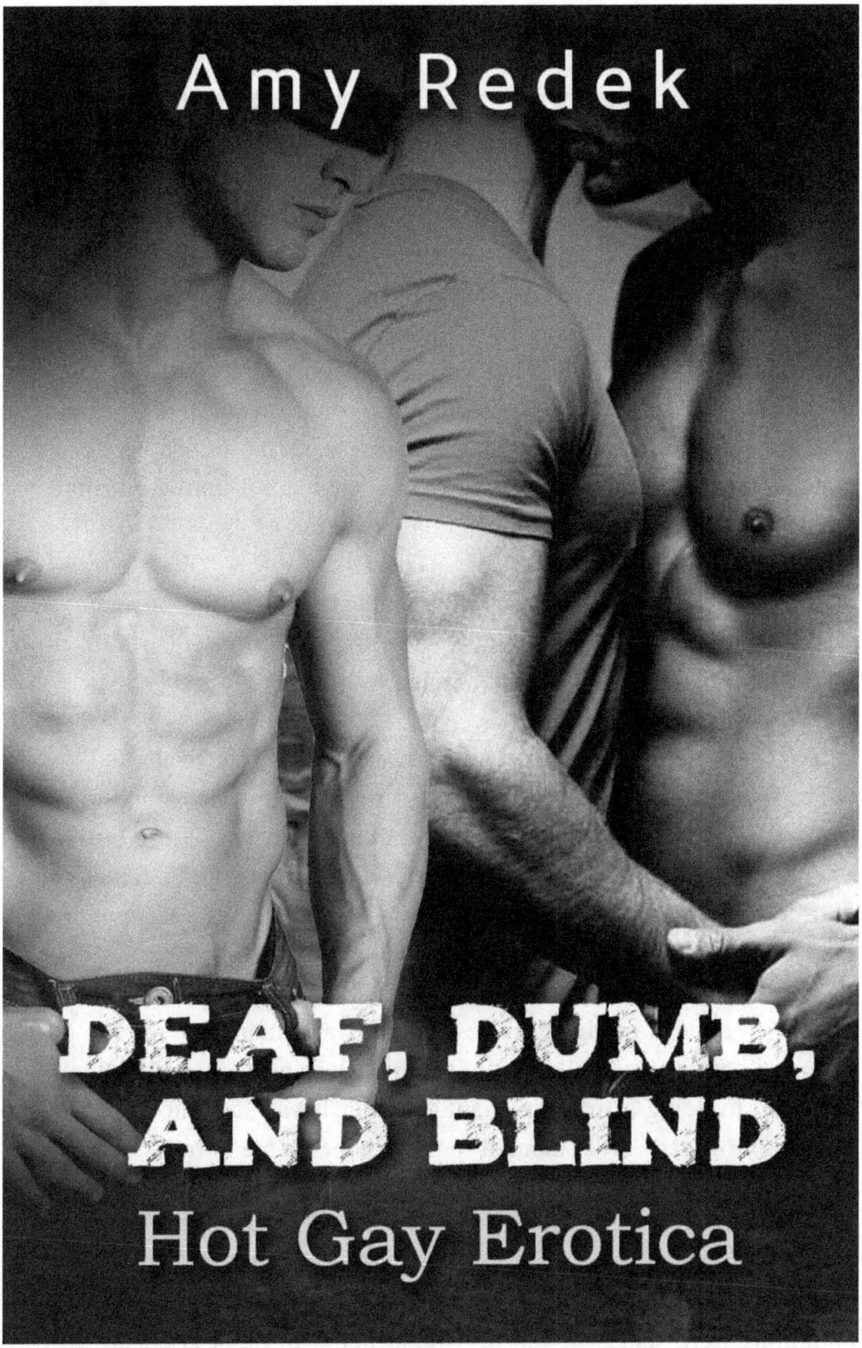

Amy Redek
DEAF, DUMB, AND BLIND
Hot Gay Erotica

I FIRST met Sergeant Bernard West, later called Bernie, and Corporal Tony Meredith when I joined the regiment as a Second Lieutenant. My name is Bryan Shorthose, and because of my surname, I was known in the cadet school as well as the officers' mess, as Sox. I was also called by that name whilst when I was at school, that being harrow before I went on to the university where I studied Military History.

I wasn't the first of our family to join the Guards; for my grandfather was a Colonel, serving in the First World War until he retired. Followed by my father who fought in the Second one. Though when the war ended, he resigned his commission, that of being a Captain, and started up his own business. Why he chose to make mannequins for retail shop windows is that I don't know, but that was what he did and made quite substantial profit out of it.

He wanted me to join him to later take over the business, but I didn't fancy that idea and opted for the army. With my degree from the university plus my family connections, I was able to join the Guards.

We lost my mother while I was in my early teens and so she never saw me on graduation day or of my passing out parade to which my father attended both. So shortly after my twenty fifth birthday, I joined my new regiment. I was assigned to be in charge of Baker squad, with Bernie being my sergeant and Tony being the corporal; though then, they were always known as sergeant and corporal.

We did training exercises, parades and man oeuvres for over a year and got on very well as a squad, and I was quite pleased when I was made up to being a full lieutenant.; though I was still known as Sox to the senior officers but lieutenant to those beneath me in rank.

***

There was trouble out in Iraq, and that was where two of our battalions were sent. Me and my squad being in the second were flown out there during my second year with the regiment. We were stationed near Khanaqin, close to the Iran border, about one hundred miles Northeast of Baghdad, to patrol the road that some insurgents were using to cause trouble in Iraq.

I'd only been out there for a week before I was called into the C.O.'s office to be told that my father had been killed in a road accident, and I was being given compassionate leave to return home to see to his burial. It was a bitter blow with me being so far away, but I went and saw to his funeral with me being the only relative left. It was sparsely attended, being mostly employees from his little factory and a few neighbors, but it went off well and I thanked each and every one that attended and later got to speak to his manager at the factory.

In spite of the death of my father, he was quite pleased when I told him that I would make him the managing director of the company and that I would give him a free hand as long as it continued to show a profit, along with a substantial raise in his own wage packet.

It was a miserable time for me, wandering around the empty house that I'd grown up in; now having lost my last living relative. The solicitor made it quite clear that all that my father had owned now belonged to me. The business, which I've already spoken about, the house and all the monies that were in the bank was now mine. But that's no consolation to losing your father who I had hoped to make him proud of me in my role in the Guards. So it wasn't long before I returned to my battalion out there in Iraq. It didn't take long to get back into the routine and learning what our role out there was.

We did not only patrol the roads, but some of the small villages just off the beaten track. It was in one of these that we ran into trouble that changed my life and a couple of others, they being my sergeant and corporal.

We were bivouacked in tents, a short distance from Khanaqin, and I was summoned to the command tent and told that I was under the command of Captain Foster who would be leading us on a patrol through a village that I could not remember with my whole life now. I relayed the order to Sergeant West and the squad was ready when we set out on that fateful morning.

Captain Foster was leading us with me bringing up the rear of this staggered column of eleven soldiers. We were roughly ten paces apart as we walked through this small narrow street between adobe-type of dwellings. Sergeant West had been called up to the front by the captain and was told to tell me that when we would left this narrow street, we were to split apart into two sections on the next road which was quite wide. He, the captain, would lead from the left while I was to follow up at the rear on the right.

The sergeant duly passed this message on to me, and I called Corporal Meredith back to pass on the instructions as to our deployment when the road would open up into this bigger street ahead of us. Meredith was still by my side when the sergeant moved forward and was about the fourth man in this irregular line when he stopped and knelt down in the dusty road and seemed to sweep the dust with his hand. Everybody kept on moving, passing him by and Corporal Meredith stopped to ask him what he had seen. They were like that when I got up to them, with the sergeant still kneeling down and the corporal standing up next to him when it happened.

There was this bloody great explosion and I felt as though I've been kicked in the head as I was blown ass over it and lost consciousness at that point in the proceedings amidst the swirling dust and debris…

If you enjoyed this sample then look for **Deaf, Dumb, and Blind**.

Also by this Author:

The Painted Sword

Cruise Control

Wild Pleasures

Lending My Beloved

Lady of Cuckolds

Lady of Pleasure

Lady Magenta

Sexually Overdosed

Meeting My Fancy Dear

Prison Sex Slave

Chasing A Shadow

The Hostel

The Island

Thirst for Drugs and Pleasure

Forgotten Identity

Grey Memories

Chronos: Time Machine

The Hard Bomber

Honeymoon Abduction

The Yacht Sins

Summer at the Villa

Practice Makes Perfect

Stranger Danger

Following Father's Footsteps

The Square Circle

The Wizard of Kos

Out in the Real World

Me, Carol and Raoul

From the Author

Check my page on Amazon and my blog for Updates and interesting info.

Author Central – http://www.amazon.com/Amy-Redek/e/B00A48NQ72
Author Blog – http://amy-redek.awesomeauthors.org/

If you enjoyed any of my books then please share the love and click like on my books in Amazon.

If you write me a review and send me an email I will send you a free book, or many.
(Just know that these emails are filtered by my publisher.)

Good news is always welcome.

One Last Thing, For Kindle Readers...

When you turn the page, Kindle will give you the opportunity to rate this book and share your thoughts on Facebook and Twitter. If you enjoyed my writings, would you please take a few seconds to let your friends know about it? Because... when they enjoy they will be grateful to you and so will I.

Thank You!

Amy Redek
amy_redek@awesomeauthors.org

About the Author

George Eliot was a famous writer, though at the time, only male authors were recognised. It was in fact the pen name of Mary Ann Evans, a female.

When I started writing, I thought that if a woman could use a male name, why, with me being male, why couldn't I use the name of a female? Though to be different, I made my writer's name from an anagram of my real name.

I wasn't the brightest spark in my school days and it was only while being in the Merchant Navy did I self-educate myself. That being mostly literature, classical music and artists, like Tolstoy, Chopin and Rembrandt. After leaving the navy, I had several jobs, finishing up by being a working boss using my own maxim that 'Management is the art of delegation.'

It's when I became self-employed that I began to write, though sadly, not many of my books can be published because of certain laws that forbid certain aspects of life. This never fazed me for I was really writing just to please myself having a wide range of the human psych.

Having written ninety stories, my only aim now is to reach one hundred. I give thanks to the publishers for at least putting some of my efforts out for others to enjoy as much as I did in the writing of them.

www.ingramcontent.com/pod-product-compliance
Lightning Source LLC
Chambersburg PA
CBHW060742180626
46819CB00001B/65